# *Mama's*
## *Deadly Secret*

KARON CURTIS

PAGE PUBLISHING, INC.
Conneaut Lake, PA

First originally published by Page Publishing 2020

ISBN 978-1-6624-1346-9 (pbk)
ISBN 978-1-6624-1347-6 (digital)

Printed in the United States of America

To Daniel and DeNajia.

# Chapter 1

Payton ran into Garrett on the way to his locker. They chat for a while about hanging out at 8 Ball to shoot pool and throw some hoops. Payton agreed and gave Garrett dap and, within minutes, was in his Jeep heading home.

Payton was beginning to dread going home. Lately, his parents have been arguing about Kennedy and her friends. Payton realized that Kennedy's stealing was causing his parents' stress, but he had no idea how to approach them about it. All he could do was pray that things would get better. When Payton got home, he ran upstairs to his room. He heard his dad yelling from his parents' room. It was beginning to feel like the norm, and Payton didn't like that...not at all.

"Kennedy must have stolen something again," he mumbled to himself. Every time their father was away on business, Kennedy would act up. Payton couldn't understand why their mom let her get away with stealing time after time. He knew one thing for sure, he was tired of it and was ready to go out and have some fun. Payton jumped in the shower, changed clothes, made himself a ham sandwich, and headed to the garage.

"Yo, G, I'm on my way over."

"Okay, cool. Where are we going?" Garrett asked.

Payton replied, "8 Ball, man, remember? You suggested it, and I haven't been there in a minute, so I'm down."

"Okay, bet. See you in a bit."

Within a few minutes, Payton pulled up at Garrett's house. Garrett jumped in the Jeep, and they headed to 8 Ball.

Garrett and Payton have been best friends since third grade. It was one of those rare occasions when students had to pair up with a schoolmate for what the school called the "buddy system." Payton and Garrett were accountable to each other on finishing homework assignments, studying, and making it to the school bus stop on time. Even though it was a nine-month term, those nine months allowed them to really get to know each other, and they became best friends.

"Yo, man, when are you gonna clean this car out? It smells like sweaty gym gear in here."

"What! How can you talk—you don't even have a car."

"That has nothing to do with what I'm saying, man. How are we supposed to have honeys up in here when it's all dirty and smelly and shit?"

"Man, whatever… I ain't ready for no honeys to be up in here anyway. I got plans."

"Yeah, whatever, man."

They reached 8 Ball and met up with their friends Alex and Cameron. As they played a game of pool, Payton noticed the cuties in the rear, playing video games. Payton's eyes were glued on the most beautiful girl he has ever seen. He knew instantly that he wanted to get to know her.

"Yo, G. Who's that cutie over there talking to Shayla?"

"Man, I don't know. Why don't you go and find out?"

"Me, nah, man. It ain't even like that. I just know that I haven't seen her in school. And since you seem to know everything and everyone, and I do mean everyone, I just thought you might have known who she was."

"Sorry to disappoint you, bro. I know I'm popular in all, but I don't know who she is, but like I said—"

"I know what you said, G. Go ahead and take your shot."

Just as Garrett finished his shot, Trey and his boys came in 8 Ball, acting rowdy. Payton could tell that they were high and were out looking for trouble as usual.

"What up, G?" said Trey. "You still hanging out with ol' church boy Watson, huh?"

"Trey, don't start. He's my friend and—"

"Yeah, but I'm your blood, and blood is thicker than water."

"What's that supposed to mean?" said Payton. "You got something to say to me, man?"

"Nah, bro, I'm just saying." Trey gave Garrett dap and nodded his boys to follow him over to where the girls were.

"Yo, G, your cousin is high as hell. What's up with that? Doesn't he know we got a game tomorrow night?" Payton asked.

"Yeah, but apparently, he doesn't care about that. He's a spoiled brat and gets high all the time. That's why I chose not to hang with him. I see him enough in school and every Sunday anyways."

"Every Sunday?"

"Yeah. After church, my mom and his mom insists on our families eating Sunday dinner together," Garrett answered.

"Yo, G, that's whack!" said Alex as he chuckled.

"I know, tell me about it. At least I get to see my little cousin Ebony. She's so cute.

They all laughed as they headed to a booth near the video games. Payton headed over to the soda bar to order some beverages for his friends. As he was waiting for the bartender, he noticed the cute girl standing a few feet away from him. He turned to the right to say hello, but no words came out. Her beauty had him in awe and left him speechless. When the bartender came, Payton allowed her to order her drink first.

"Ladies first," he said with a smile as he looked at her.

"Thank you," she replied.

"You're welcome."

"You come here a lot?" she asked.

"Pretty much. There's not a lot to do in this town, except go to the movies, mall, skating rink, and 8 Ball." He chuckled.

"Oh, I see. Well, thanks for the cut. I really appreciate it."

"No problem," said Payton.

She grabbed her soda off the counter and walked back to where her friends were. Payton watched her as she made her way back to the table and sat down. He noticed that Trey jumped into the empty space next to her and started talking to her. Trey then made eye contact with Payton and in a lip-synch motion said, "She's mine." Payton turned around, ordered a pitcher of soda for his table, and went back to his booth.

# Chapter 2

As Payton was getting his things ready for the basketball game, Kennedy busted into his room and sat on his bed. Kennedy had no problem making herself known when it came to her brother and his room. The excitement of busting in his room whenever she liked made her feel grown although Payton was quick to put Kennedy back in her place.

"Girl, can't you knock? I thought I told you about busting in my room without knocking."

"Yeah, I know but I need a favor…like really quick."

"Oh really, and what might that be?"

"Well, you know I like watching you play ball and dunk and all that shit, right?"

"Girl, watch your mouth. You gotta find new friends because the ones you have right now are a bad influence on you."

"Whatever! Mom says the same thing. My girls know how to have fun though, so why would I stop hanging out with them? And plus, we're freshman so we gotta at least live up to the 'fresh.'"

"And get in trouble?"

"Not that much trouble."

"Oh really. Well then, how come Mom and Dad were yelling yesterday about you stealing again?"

"What! I haven't stole anything since like Thanksgiving weekend, so I don't know what the hell you're talking about."

"Whatever, Kennedy. And watch your mouth, girl."

"I'm serious, Payton… I'm not lying."

"Whatever! So what's the favor?"

"Well, I wanna go to the movies with my boy Jake, but I know Mom won't let me. So can you just tell her that I'm gonna ride to the game with you, and you can drop me off at the movies on your way to your game?"

"So you want me to lie to Mom about your whereabouts? I don't think so."

"But kids do it all the time, Payton. And I know mom will believe you."

"Girl, get outa here before I tell Ma that you're scheming again."

Upset and disappointed, Kennedy stomped out of the room. Payton gathered the rest of his things, ran downstairs, grabbed a Gatorade, and made his way to the game. When Payton got to the locker room, he noticed that Trey wasn't there and wondered if Trey got busted last night.

"Yo, Garrett, where's your cousin?"

"Man, I don't know. He called me thirty minutes ago talking about he's on his way. He's so damn slow and seems to have a problem with keeping time."

"Well, he better be here. We're gonna need him tonight."

"I thought you didn't like him."

"I never said that... Why would you think that?"

"P, you're always rash toward him, and you don't really say much to him."

"Dude, your cousin smokes way too much weed and sells it on the DL like no one knows what he's doing. That's not the lifestyle I care to be around. And the sad thing is, he's a smart guy... I just don't understand him. Drugs are no good, and they sure ain't gonna help me get a scholarship. Real talk, though, he seems cool, but his ways are jacked up. Know what I mean?"

"Yeah, man. I know exactly what you mean. His mom doesn't understand either. And it hurts her a lot because his little sister really looks up to him."

"Man, that's deep. Guess she's gonna have to find another role model, huh?"

Just then, Trey comes busting into the locker room like he's the man and he's the whole team by himself. The team realized that Trey was no where near ready to play ball and not focused on the game.

"Hey, girlies, what the hell is up?"

"You're late again, Mr. Thomas," said Coach. "You will warm the bench for the first quarter."

"Coach, really? I had to take my mom and little sister all the way across town, Coach."

"Trey, you know the rules. If you continue to break them, you have to suffer the consequences. And next time, Mr. Thomas, call me so I can turn the roster in on time."

"I called Garrett."

"Garrett isn't the coach. I am. Call the coach next time. Thank you! Now get your gear on and get focused."

"Thanks a lot, cuz. You could have told coach I was running late."

"True, but you still would have been bench-warming, so it wouldn't have made a difference."

Payton chuckled as Trey walked past them in disgust. He cut his eyes at Payton as if it was Payton's fault that he had to warm the bench the first quarter.

During the end of the second quarter, Payton notices the pretty girl he saw at 8 Ball. She's a cheerleader! What! He couldn't believe it was her. *She's a student here*, he thought to himself. He couldn't believe how beautiful she looked in her uniform. With his attention on her, he lost the ball and was taken out of the game. In disgust, he plopped himself down in his seat next to Garrett, not realizing that the opposing team was now up by six points.

"Yo, Payton. What are you doing out there? Coach is pissed."

"I know. He gave me the evil eye."

"So what's going on, you sick?"

"Nah, G. You remember the girl I asked you about at 8 Ball last night?"

"No, not really. I was too busy beating you out of five dollars."

"Well, anyway, she's here man…cheering. And when I saw her, I lost my concentration."

"What, P! That's crazy. Ain't no girl ever made you lose your concentration."

"Man, I know, but she is absolutely gorgeous!"

"Well, I tell you what. If you don't concentrate, we're gonna lose, and you know we need to win this game to be in the tourney, got me? So, my man, get it together!"

"I will, G, I will."

After about ten minutes, Coach Monroe called Payton back into the game. Before Payton checked back into the game, the coach stopped him at the table to put a bug in his ear.

Coach must have said something really good to Payton because right at the half-time buzzer, Payton shot a three-pointer, putting the Mighty Cougars within three points of the opposing team. The crowd got excited and jumped to their feet. His teammates rushed to him on the court as if they won the game. The referees blew their whistles to move the players off the court. Payton sat down to catch his breath and wipe the sweat off his forehead. As the team headed to the locker room, the cheerleaders ran to center court to do a dance routine. Payton didn't want to miss this, so he took his time heading to the locker room. He watched her for a few minutes…just enough time to realize that he *liked* what he saw.

In the third and fourth quarters, the Cougars took charge and had no mercy on the Jaguars. The Cougars played like a team, scoring and assisting each other, even Trey and Payton played like they were in harmony.

After winning the game, the team made their way back to the locker room with excitement. On the way to the locker room, a man that Payton has never seen before stopped him and told him that he played a good game. Payton was a bit puzzled as to why the security guard stopped him. He didn't know the security guard nor has he ever had any encounters with him.

"Great game, guys," said Coach. "We almost had a scare there in the third quarter, but you all pulled through as always."

"Mr. Watson, what's going on with you? You took your eyes off the ball in the second and third quarter. You forced two turnovers. Are you okay?"

"Sorry, Coach, it won't happen again."

"It better not. And you, Mr. Clayton, you missed three free throws tonight. That's unacceptable. You're one of my best free-throwers, and we can't have you missing them. Please don't tell me the holiday break is making you guys lazy? Damn, it just started. I don't want to have you guys practicing every day, but I will if I have to. So, guys, work with me here, okay?"

"That won't be necessary, Coach," replied Alex.

"And, Mr. Greene, nice job on the boards. Great job rebounding."

"Thanks, Coach," replied Cameron.

"Okay. Well, listen, go out and have some fun tonight. No practice tomorrow. It's Sunday, and I want to see y'all at church. We will have practice on Monday, ten o'clock sharp. We got game two on Tuesday. And, girls, please be on time," he continued as he looked toward Trey.

Payton chuckled, which infuriated Trey and made him even hotter.

The players showered. Payton and his friends changed into their chill gear at school, jumped in his Jeep, and headed to the movies.

"So what's playing tonight, guys?"

"Not sure. Let me check my phone," said Garrett.

"Man, that old phone. Is Santa getting you a new phone for Christmas?" Cam asked.

"Man, shut the fuck up! Santa knows what's up, plus, I've been good this year…real good!" replied Garrett as he smirked to his boys.

"Oh, so what you mean is…you ain't been getting any, huh?"

"Man, be quiet," said Garrett.

"Man, what's playing?" yelled Alex, annoyed with all the idle talk.

"The Hangover," replied Garrett.

"Fellas, the previews looked funny as hell. We should go see that shit for real," said Alex.

"Let's do it then," replied Payton.

Payton drove into the parking lot. He and his friends jumped out of the Jeep and headed into the theater. They proceeded to purchase their tickets, popcorn, and candy.

"Yo, Cam, isn't that your cousin Shayla over there?" said Alex.

"Man, she ain't my cousin."

"Well, why y'all always call each other cuz?"

"Because our families are close like that, man. And my mom's told me to look after her like she's my cousin. Where she at?"

"Over there, man, playing video games. Man, she sure looking good from behind."

"Chill, Alex, that's my cuz. And why you sound like you wanna get at her? Don't you go with Brie?"

"I'm just saying she's looking good. And yes, Brie is my girl, but she ain't here right now. And you know I like the honeys."

"Well, you can forget about Shayla because she won't do her crew like that."

"Whatever, man!"

"But on the real, man, those multiple honey days are over for me. I can only handle one chick at a time. Plus, two girls means two paychecks, and I ain't tryin' to work no two jobs."

Payton and his crew gathered all their goodies, paid for them, and entered the theater room to find seats. As they were heading up the stairs, the lights went out. They finally made their way to the top row but not before Garrett tripped over his foot and almost fell. They continued up the stairs to the top row and heard girls laughing.

"Who's that laughing, G?" asked Payton.

"My cousin Shayla and her crew," replied Cam.

"Hey, what's up, Shayla," said Payton.

"Nothing. Y'all just need to sit down and be quiet because the movie is about to start, and I ain't up for no interruptions, feel me?"

"Damn, girl," said Alex.

Shayla turned her head around and rolled her eyes at Alex. And someone in the theater made a big *ssshhhh* sound.

The boys obeyed Shayla and sat down. After the movie, the house lights came on. The boys got up to leave the theater, but the girls stayed to watch the bloopers. As Payton was going down the stairs, he turned around to say good night to the girls, and immediately, his eyes were fixated on her. He couldn't believe she was sitting a row in front of him, and he didn't notice. She was an arm reach away from him, and he didn't even know. He thought to himself,

*Wow, I've seen this girl three times in two days, and I still don't know her name.*

Tiffany noticed Payton staring at her and couldn't do anything but smile. Payton smiled back. He thought for a second to say good night, but his boys were acting silly and rushing him down the stairs. As he turned the corner wall to exit, he looked up to where she was sitting… He *had* to get one last look at her before he went home.

# Chapter 3

Tuesday finally arrived, and Payton was ready to win another game. He stayed home and rested most of the day. Besides surfing the net and texting Garrett, he was also thinking about her. He wondered what she was doing and thought of ways to get her number. But then he thought about the vow he made to himself: *Stay focused on senior year, man. You got things to accomplish!*

Payton put on his sweatpants, ran downstairs to grab an apple, and rushed to the game. As he entered the gym, he noticed the crowd was larger than the first game. *Oh, it's on*, he thought to himself. He was getting excited and couldn't wait to play. Payton made his way to the locker room to change into his basketball jersey and shorts.

The Mighty Cougars played an awesome game. They beat the Bulldogs by seven points and were closer to the championship game. As the team made their way to the locker room, Payton noticed the security guard staring at him. He tried to avoid him by walking faster, but the security guard caught up with him.

"I must say, young man, you can really play."

"Thanks. Do I know you?"

"Not yet. But anyway, great game!"

Officer Brown walked away to tend to the crowds, trying to exit the gym. Payton was left standing there, wondering who this officer was and why he kept making it a point to say something to him. Paris noticed the officer talking to Payton and decided to text her brother.

"Bro, who was that cop?"

"Idk, but he was at the game Saturday too."

"What did he say?"

"Nothing, just that I played a good game."

"Well, did you notice a ring bro? That brother looked kinda good from where I'm sitting."

"See you later, Paris…LOL. Tell Ma I'm going to 8 Ball with Garrett."

The team showered and changed into their weekend gear. Payton and Garrett jumped in his Jeep and headed to 8 Ball. Alex rode with Cameron in his car. When they arrived, they proceeded to the rear of 8 Ball and began shooting hoops.

"Great game, y'all. Way to rebound, Cam. You rebound like that for the championship game this weekend, and we're sure to win."

"Thanks, Cappie," said Cameron. "Now what you gonna do about Trey's lateness?"

"Fire him."

They all laughed.

"Now, Payton," said Garrett, "you really gonna do that to my cuz."

"Nah, man, I'm just joking."

"A'ight!"

The boys were interrupted when Shayla ran into the gym to tell Garrett that Trey was messing with her friend.

"Garrett, you need to come out here and control your silly ass cousin."

"Why? What's he doing?"

"He's messing with my girl, and I'm about to slap the hell out of him."

"Damn," said Garrett. "Why can't that boy just chill out."

Garrett followed Shayla back into the pool hall to see what was going on. Payton, Alex, and Cameron looked at each other, dropped the basketballs, and followed Garrett into the pool hall. As they approached the booth where the girls were sitting, they could see that the girls were agitated with Trey. He was being loud and obnoxious, squeezing himself into the booth, where obviously, he couldn't fit.

Trey was brushing up against the girl, getting all up in her face as if he was going to kiss her. She tried to push Trey away with her hands, but he was getting more pushy.

"Oh, c'mon, girl, you know you wanna kiss me."

"Boy, I don't even know you. Can you please just leave me alone?"

"Not until I get my kiss."

Just then, Garrett and Cameron approached Trey at the table. Alex and Payton stood nearby as if they were on watch for Trey's crew.

"Trey, leave the girl alone," said Garrett. "She doesn't want to be bothered."

"G, man, please. Step with that mess. You're gay anyway, so you ain't got nothing to say to me."

Garrett's friends were surprised by what Trey said. They knew Trey was simply blowing smoke. The girls were surprised and shook their heads in disbelief.

"Gay! What! Boy, I will kick your ass up in here."

Trey turned around steaming and stared at Garrett with fire in his eyes. He slammed his fist on the table and stood up to approach Garrett. The girls quickly moved from the booth, but Tiffany didn't move fast enough. Alex and Payton moved closer to the table. As Tiffany tried to get up from the table, Payton noticed it was her again. He was speechless but felt the urge to protect her. Payton reached out his hand for her to grab it. But Trey was quick and stretched out his arm to stop her from getting up as he continued to cuss out Garrett. She helplessly fell back down in the chair with a fearful look on her face.

"Now what did you say, boy?"

"I ain't your boy, Trey. And the young lady said to leave her alone, so why don't you do just that?"

"And who's gonna make me?"

"Trey, chill," said Payton. "You ain't gotta go there. Just calm down and let her out."

Trey pushed Garrett out of his way and stepped to Payton. Garrett stumbled backward.

"Ain't nobody talking to you, church boy, so mind your damn business before I kick your ass too."

"Whatever, Trey!"

"Yeah, whatever, you punk-ass nigga. You might as well get security 'cause you're gonna need him once I'm through with you."

Nikki and Desi went to get security. Shayla stayed near the booth, refusing to leave Tiffany alone with Trey.

"I'm about tired of your threats, Trey. You don't scare me. Just leave her alone."

Trey shoulder bumped Payton as he sat back down. He grabbed Tiffany's forearm and attempted to pull her closer to him.

"Get your hands off me!" she yelled as she tried to remove his hand.

He didn't budge. Payton had seen enough at this point. He gave Garrett that "I'm done with his shit" look, stepped to the table, and pulled Trey out of the booth. Trey's boys quickly stepped to Payton as if they were going to jump him, but Payton's crew was right on their tails. No one made a move.

"Man, I can see you're high as a kite, so I'm not gonna fuck with you right now. But I think it would be best if you and your crew left…now!"

Payton let go of Trey with a forceful push that made Trey take a few steps back.

"Whatever, man," said Trey. "Yo, let's get outa this lame place. She ain't even cute."

By this time, security came to diffuse the commotion and break up the crowd. The security guards escorted the boys outside to get the full story. Payton was surprised to see that the security guard was the same guy from the game. The girls put their coats on and followed the boys outside. They all watched the security guards talk to Trey and his crew near the patrol cars.

"Hey, G, that's the same guy that stopped me at the game earlier tonight."

"Which one?"

"The one on the right, right there, talking to Trey."

"What! Are you sure?"

"Very sure… How ironic is that? Three times in two days… That's kinda odd."

"Payton, man, maybe he just likes his job."

They laughed.

The officer adjusted his hat and started walking toward Payton and Garrett. Trey's friends stood nearby, watching all the action and talking smack about how Trey would have kicked some ass. Payton ignored them. He turned his head and noticed that Alex and Cameron were keeping the girls company. He then noticed that Tiffany was on the phone, but her lips weren't moving. To Payton, she looked as if she was crying. He wanted to go to her and see if she was all right. She looked helpless, and he didn't like seeing her like that, even if he didn't know her yet. As soon as Payton started to walk over to her, the officer stopped him in his tracks.

"Excuse me, son. I'm Officer Brown. Hey, you're the badass b-ball player. You're quite good."

"Thank you, sir."

"Well, I believe I got all the necessary information that I need for the incident report. Listen, this young man is pretty wasted. And at his age, I should lock his ass up. We're going to take him downtown. Do any of you know him?"

"Yes," said Garrett. "He's my cousin. I'll call my aunt to let her know what's going on."

"That's not necessary, son. He's not under arrest or anything yet, but it could come to that. Why don't you give me her number, and I'll take care of it?"

"Okay, cool. It's 555-7248. Thank you, Officer."

"Thank you. What's your aunt's name?"

"Teresa Thomas."

"Great! I'll give your aunt a call once we're downtown. Now you young men enjoy the rest of your evening."

"We will, Officer. Thank you," replied Garrett.

"Officer Brown. Did you get a statement from the young lady as well?" asked Payton.

"Sure did. Ms. Tiffany is calling her dad to come pick her up." *So that's her name,* Payton thought to himself. "You guys should stay here with the girls until her father arrives. And then go home and get some rest for the tournament. I'm rooting for you, Cougars."

Officer Brown and his partner got into his car and drove off. Payton and Garrett watched the car as it drove off and noticed that Trey's eyes were glued on Payton.

"Yo, G, did you see how Trey was staring at me man?"

"Yup. You better watch your back, bro.

"Who you telling?"

Their conversation was cut short by a soft tap on Payton's shoulder. Payton turned around and was face-to-face with beauty. He was mesmerized. It was the pretty girl from the movie theater, the lovely girl that made him lose his concentration during the game. Garrett watched the squad car drive away. When he couldn't see the squad car anymore, he turned around to see who Payton was talking to.

"Excuse me," she said. "I just wanted to thank you both for what y'all did back there. I really appreciate it."

"You're welcome. And I'm sorry for what happened. Are you okay?"

"I apologize too," said Garrett. "Trey is my cousin, and I'm really sorry you had to endure his ignorance."

"It's not your fault, and yes, I'm okay. I just really want to go home now, and my dad isn't picking up his phone. Do you know what street this is… I need to get an Uber ride…like right now."

"Well, if you like, I can take you home," said Payton.

"Uhhh, I'm not too sure about that. Uber will be just fine."

"My man P will make sure you get home okay. He's a really good guy," said Garrett. "And why waste money when he has a ride?"

She looked at Payton with a hesitant smile. "Well, if you really don't mind."

Payton looked straight into her eyes. "I don't mind at all. G, you'll be okay riding home with Cam?"

"Sure, man. I'll see you Thursday at practice."

They gave each other dap and Garrett ran over to Cam and Alex who were keeping the girls warm in bear hugs.

"I really appreciate this. Thank you so much. So what does P stand for?"

"Well, it's actually Payton. My boys call me P. I'm parked in back. You ready?"

"Yes! I'm Tiffany by the way."

"That's a very nice name."

"Thank you."

Payton led Tiffany to the parking lot. He opened the passenger door for her and gently shut the door behind her. He eased his way into the driver's seat, thankful that he listened to Garrett and got his Jeep cleaned. The scent was nice and manly. He hoped Cam didn't mind taking Garrett home, but that was far from his mind at this moment.

"What's your address? I'll put it in my GPS."

"Cool. It's 822 Samuel Ct."

"Samuel Ct. Haven't heard of it. Is that where they're building those new homes?"

"Yeah, but I don't know which direction it's in from here."

"No problem at all," said Payton. "My GPS will get us there."

"Not sure why my dad bought a house anyway. We never stay in one place long enough."

"Maybe he has a different plan this time."

"Maybe, but I know my dad, and he gets bored...quick."

"So how come I haven't seen you in school?"

"Hmmm. Good question."

"I think so too. Usually, students have to attend school to participate in any sports."

"But I don't play any sports."

"You cheer, that's a sport now."

"Oh really, didn't know that."

"Yep, it is, so am I going to get an answer tonight?"

They laughed.

"Well, we were supposed to move here in August, so I could start school in September. I tried out for the cheer squad, made it, but then my dad had to delay the move until December. So he called the school to make sure I would still be able to transfer after Thanksgiving. They said yes, and here I am."

"Really? Thanks...for all that."

"Well, you did ask."

"You're right, I did." They laughed. "So you've been going to Caldwell High since December?"

"Yup."

"No way. I know a new face when I see one, and I haven't seen yours."

"Well, I've seen you in my social studies class."

"No way! How come I haven't seen you?"

"Maybe because that girl Keisha was all up in your face."

"Ahhh, Keisha. She and I are just friends now."

"Now?"

"Yeah. We dated last year."

"Wow! Now I see why she is always one step behind you, like a stalker."

"Huh, not. She knows I'm staying focused this year. It's my senior year, and my plan is to pass all my finals and get a good scholarship. So how come you didn't say anything to me?"

"Like what?"

"Like hi…"

"I was into my schoolwork."

"Sure you were."

They chuckled.

"By the way, this is a nice Jeep. Is this a Wrangler?" She wanted to get off the subject of relationships quick.

"No, it's a Jeep Cherokee. I love it because it's big and tough, just like me," he continued as he smiled at her.

"Oh really!" she said with a chuckle.

"And here we are," said Payton as he drove up the driveway.

"Thank you so much, Payton. Garrett was right, I see. You are a nice guy. I really appreciate you driving me home and what you did at 8 Ball."

"No problem. And I'll tell Keisha you said what's up."

"You better not."

They laughed at the thought.

"Now that's a nice car," Payton said as he nodded his head toward the black shiny BMW parked in front of the house.

"Yeah, that's my dad's baby."

"Sweet!"

"Well, I better get inside before my dad comes out and embarrasses me."

Payton got out of his Jeep and walked around to the passenger side to help Tiffany out of the Jeep. He walked her to the porch and made sure she got in the house okay. They quickly said good night to each other, and Payton made his way back to his Jeep. He turned around and noticed she was still smiling as she shut the door. As he jumped in his Jeep, he felt excited about Tiffany and the possibilities that could be. But just as quickly as the thought entered his mind, it quickly escaped his mind. He knew he didn't have time for a girlfriend, not now. He just told her what his plans were, and he had to stick to them. But then again, something about Tiffany was special, and he knew that he needed to find a way to fit her into his plans... somehow.

*****

"Hey, Dad, it's me!" yelled Tiffany as she walked into the house.

"Hey, sugarplum. How was the game? Who won?"

"It was great. We won. You should come to a game dad. The team is awesome!"

"Awww, I'll think about it. I'd rather just go to see my sugarplum cheer."

"You know you don't have to, dad, that was Mom's love. I don't expect you to fill her shoes that way. I know cheering isn't really your thing."

"It really isn't, but no one's there to cheer you on."

"Dad, it's okay. I'm good."

"Oh really. So why do you seem a bit agitated?"

"Well, it's definitely not about that. Some guy at 8 Ball was acting like an idiot," she replied as she sat down on the couch.

"What? Did he bother you?"

"He was bothering me and my friends. I called you to come get me, but you didn't pick up your phone. Were you out?"

"You didn't call me, baby. I had my phone with me all night, in this house, and it didn't ring."

"Really? Are you sure?" Tiffany asked as she looked through her calls.

"Absolutely," Mr. Campbell replied with his eyes glued to the flat-screen TV.

"Oh my goodness, dad, I have no idea who I was calling... This is not even your number!" she said with a laugh.

"Tiff, that's not funny, and I'm not going to keep telling you to put me on speed dial. My number and 911 should be your first two contacts. You hungry?"

"Sorry, Dad. I'll make sure I do that tonight. No, I had pizza earlier. So no date for you tonight?"

"Nah, not tonight. We went out last night, plus I'm kinda tired and wanted to relax tonight alone."

"Mmmm, hmmm."

They laughed. "Ms. Crystal is keeping you busy, huh?"

"You can say that again, sugarplum. She's showing me a lot of the town, and I'm almost sure I know where every steak house is."

They laughed.

"I'm gonna go take a shower and go to bed. Shayla wants me to go to the mall with her tomorrow after practice. Would that be okay?"

"Fine with me, baby girl. Shayla seems like a nice young lady."

"She is, Dad."

Tiffany gave her dad a hug and kiss good night and exited the room.

"Sugarplum?"

"Yes?"

"So how did you get home?"

"Oh, a friend from school," she said as she ran up the stairs smiling.

"Oh okay, well, good night, love."

"Good night, Daddy. Love you."

"Love you more."

Tiffany ran upstairs with a big smile on her face. Even with the unexpected and irritating Trey messing with her at 8 Ball, she found solace in thinking about Payton and his gorgeous smile. Although the thought of being with Payton was nice, she knew that her heart was with her current boyfriend, Jarod. She and Jarod decided to stay a couple even though she moved to Virginia. It hadn't really dawned on them of how a long-distance relationship would work. All they knew was that they loved each other, and no matter what, they would be together. Her mixed emotions prompted her to call Shayla before she took a shower.

"Hey, Shayla, what's up?"

"Nothing, girl, how are you? You home?"

"I'm okay. Just got in the house."

"Cool. My mom would have taken you home, girl. Why did you leave so soon?"

"I just wanted to get out of there. That Trey is a piece of work. I'll have something for his ass if he messes with me again."

They laughed.

"Yes, he got issues. I mean, we all got issues, but he really got issues. He needs to stop smoking that mess before he gets kicked off the team or worse…locked up."

"I'm surprised he's still on the team."

"Me too. He knows when to smoke, though. He's smart like that, but it's gonna catch up with him soon. Mark my words."

"You're right, Shayla."

"Well, I'm glad you're okay. I saw you with Payton. What's up with that?"

"Nothing. He offered to take me home, and I accepted. Sorry for not letting you know."

"Girl, don't sweat it. My mom took like thirty minutes to come get us anyway."

"Dag, what, she drove the speed limit all the way, huh?"

"Probably. So what's going on with you and Payton?"

"What do you mean? I just met him tonight, but he does seem nice."

"You know what I mean, girl. That's the guy you told me about Saturday, how he let you order your drink first, remember?"

"Yeah, I remember, Shayla, and I have a boyfriend."

"Yeah, a boyfriend all the way in Jersey, enjoying his freshman year in college. Well, just so you know, so many girls tried to talk to Payton ever since school started, and he politely brushed them off. And his ex, Keisha, girl, she ain't even trying to let him go. She's never too far away from him… She's like a leech."

"Really? That's crazy."

"Yeah, well, she supposed to be with some dude from Washington High now."

"Wow. Does Payton still like her?"

"I doubt it. That was last year girl. I'm sure he's over it by now. Anyway, Payton's focus this year is on his game, girl. Word is that he's going pro."

"Really? Well, he sure is a good player."

"Yup, but he told Garrett that going pro is not what he wants right now. Did he ask you for your number?"

"Nope."

See what I mean? He doesn't want to get involved with anyone now. Just be friends with him and hang out. Plus, you got Jarod."

"Yeah, I sure do. Jarod is my baby."

"Girl, how you gonna handle senior year and a long-distance relationship?"

"I don't know. Oooh, that's Jarod calling me now. Talk to you later, girl."

"No doubt. Good night."

"Okay, good night, Shayla."

# Chapter 4

Officer Brown cuffs Trey and puts him in the back seat of his cruiser. He and his partner jump in the front seat of the car and take off. The officer starts heading toward the precinct but suddenly takes a right turn away from the precinct.

"So what do you think we should do with this one?" asked Officer Brown.

"Man, I don't know," said the other officer. "You told me to come down here, and I'm down here trying to figure out what the hell you're doing."

"Relax, bro. I'll drop you off in a few."

"Cool," said the other officer.

"Yo, Officer, where the hell are we going?" Trey asked as he leaned toward the front of the cruiser. "This isn't the way to the brick."

"Watch your mouth, young boy. You're addressing an officer in uniform."

"An officer in uniform, man, please, you're just some punk ass security officers. Let me outa here."

"You ain't going anywhere. We need to talk."

"Awww, shit. Damn." Trey fell back into his seat and looked out the window. Officer Brown stopped the car.

"Okay, man, you can get out here," said Officer Brown as he stopped the car. "I'll get with you later."

"Cool." The other officer jumped out of the car and left. Officer Brown turned around with a mean look on his face. He reached in the glove compartment and pulled out a gun. He pointed his gun at

Trey. Trey was shocked and didn't know what to do. Officer Brown got out of the car and opened Trey's door.

"Get your ass up here in the front seat. We need to talk."

Trey didn't say anything. He willingly got out of the back seat and jumped into the front seat.

"Now, let's talk," said Officer Brown as he pulled off.

A mild-toned Trey responded, "Talk about what?"

"I need to know more about your boy Payton."

"He's not my boy, and I don't really know him that well. We just go to the same damn school and happen to play ball together."

"Y'all go to the same high school and y'all play ball together, so I know you know him more than you say you do."

"Whatever, man!"

"Whatever. Boy, I will bust a cap in your ass," said Officer Brown as he put the gun to Trey's head. "All you are is a wannabe tough guy, ain't ya? Now you're gonna give me something on him, and that's all to it. Do you understand me?"

"What do you want to know?" Trey asked nervously.

"Everything."

"Listen, Officer, Payton is not one of my boys. I can't stand the dude. I put up with him sometimes because he's my cousin's boy. And can you please put the gun down… You're making me nervous."

Officer Brown put the gun under his seat.

"Yea, but I'm sure you know where he lives, works—"

"I have no idea where he lives…never been to the asshole's house. But I think he works at one of those senior living homes."

"Oh really?"

"Yes."

"Which one?"

"Now how am I supposed to know that? I'm not into the guy like that."

"You better not be pulling my leg. If I find out you're giving me bull, I'll make sure you never play ball again."

"Hah, so now you're threatening me?"

"Call it what you want, shithead. So here's the deal. You're gonna call or text your cousin and get me the name of that home…

You hear me? I need to know, ASAP. If I don't hear from you by tomorrow, this little incident tonight is going on record. Got it?"

"Yeah, I got it. Can I go now?"

"No. Put my number in your phone. When you get the info, text it to me."

"Why you sweating that sucker?"

"None of your damn business. Just text me the info by tomorrow."

"Sure thing, Officer Brown, sure thing."

Officer Brown reached over to Trey's seat and uncuffed him. He pulled up in front of a bus stop and let Trey out.

"Tomorrow," he yelled at Trey through the window. Officer Brown sped off and left Trey standing at the bus stop.

# Chapter 5

Christmas was quickly approaching, and Mrs. Watson was getting excited for the holidays. The Watson's house was decorated in Christmas decor inside and out. Mrs. Watson designed the holiday decor herself, and every year, her family was amazed at how beautiful the house looked. Christmas was her family's favorite holiday. They looked forward to trimming the tree, making ginger bread cookies, watching all the holiday shows, and especially shopping for one another.

As Mr. Watson made his way into the kitchen, he kissed his wife on the cheek. He loved his wife and his family very much, but lately, he and his wife have been at each other's neck. He was just about fed up with all the fussing and arguing. Arguing was not something he wanted to come home to after working out of town. He simply wanted to enjoy spending time with his family.

The children realized that something wasn't right. Payton and Paris heard their parents arguing on more than one occasion but didn't want to address it. For it was grown folks' business, and Mr. Watson told them time and time again to stay out of grown folks' business.

"Hey, Payton, what's up with Mom and Dad?" asked Paris as they sat in the family room.

"What do you mean?" Payton stepped behind the Christmas tree to turn on the tree lights.

"I heard them arguing last weekend about some phone calls."

"What phone calls? They probably were arguing about Kennedy and her extracurricular activities."

"Funny, Payton," said Kennedy. "I have no extra activities. I haven't stolen anything since like the summer." She smirked, knowing she was lying.

"Try Thanksgiving, Kennie," said Paris. "Well, they were sure arguing over something."

"Well, it wasn't over me. Maybe it was over one of y'all trifling asses. I'm not the only one with issues. Y'all got issues too," whined Kennedy.

"True, but we know how to handle ours," said Paris. "And you better watch your mouth up in here. You ain't grown."

"Really? So how come you're twenty-two years old, without a job, and still living at your mama's house?"

"Oh, snap, she got you, Paris," said Payton.

"That's not an issue. It's a situation. And you don't need to be concerned with that," Paris retorted.

"Whatever, Paris! Just leave me alone," Kennedy snapped.

"Well, ladies," said Payton, "I'm going to change and go to work. See y'all later."

"You working today? I thought it was your day off?" asked Paris.

"It was. I'm taking David's shift so he can take mine this weekend. I can't work this weekend because of the tournament. Plus we're having our office Christmas party tonight, and I want to be there."

"So y'all gonna have seventy-year-olds doing the electric slide in wheelchairs, huh?" said Kennedy as she laughed uncontrollably.

"Not funny, Kennie," said Paris. "Don't let me have to tell Ma on you, again."

Payton shook his head in disbelief. He couldn't believe some of the things that came out of Kennedy's mouth.

"So, Paris, you're not going out with Derek tonight?" asked Payton.

"Nope, he pissed me off at the club last week, so he's off my dating list right now. I'm staying in tonight...gotta submit a few more job apps...you know how that is."

"Yes, I do, but I also know that your butt needs a job...soon." They all laughed.

Payton left his sisters in the family room and headed to work. Kennedy continued to watch TV. As Paris headed to her room, she heard her parents arguing again. She didn't like it when they argued. Paris could remember that not too long ago, everything seemed so perfect at home. Now things were different, and Paris didn't know why. Paris was tempted to knock on the door to see what the problem was but decided against it. She stood near their bedroom door to eavesdrop.

"Baby, I am telling you the truth. I don't know who's calling the house. When I pick up, I hear nothing. Why don't we just change the number?"

"Honey, I'm not changing the number again. I changed it last month when I came home, and I'm not changing it this month. Do you get crank calls when I'm not here?"

"No. Why?" Jessica hesitantly replied.

"Because something ain't right, baby. There's something you're not telling me, sweetheart, and I would really appreciate it if you would be honest and tell me what's going on."

Mr. Watson gave his wife that "I don't know anymore" look and went to watch television in the sitting area. A tear rolled down Mrs. Watson's face as she walked into the bathroom to breathe. She didn't like lying to her husband, but she was tired of all the fighting that was going on. How was she to tell her husband that yes, she has been getting crank calls, that someone's been calling late at night and breathing into the phone. She just didn't see a way to explain to her husband that she may know who the crank caller was. There was no way her husband, who was always understanding, would completely understand that. Mrs. Watson washed her face and headed downstairs to spend time with Kennedy.

"Hey, Mom."

"Hey, honey, what are you watching?"

"*Good Times* marathon."

"Yes. I love that show."

"Me too. This is the Christmas episode where they have a party."

"Oooh. I like this one."

Mrs. Watson and Kennedy quietly watched *Good Times* together until Kennedy fell asleep on the floor. Mrs. Watson picked her up and laid her on the couch. She turned off the television and went upstairs to get ready for bed. She then realized she hadn't seen Paris since dinner, so she stopped in Paris' room to say good night.

"Knock, knock," she said as she opened the door. "Hey, baby, how you doing?"

"Oh, hey, Ma. I'm doing okay…just filling out some applications. I actually got an e-mail back from one company, and they want to see me next Tuesday at ten."

"That's good, sweetie. I'll keep my fingers crossed."

"Thanks, Mom."

"You're welcome, sweetie. Don't stay up too late. Your body needs to rest too."

"I know, Ma. I'll be done soon. Is everything okay with you and Dad?"

"Yeah, baby, everything is okay. Good night now. Listen, why don't you join me and Kennie tomorrow. I'm taking her to work with me. Then we're going to have lunch and finish our Christmas shopping."

"That would be awesome, Mom, thanks."

"Okay, Paris, good night. And please clean up this room and your bathroom. Your cousins will be here Saturday morning. I also need you to tidy up the guest rooms as well."

"Okay, Mom. Will do. Nate and Arianna will be here just in time for the party."

"Yup! And you know they'll want to go…really bad."

"I bet."

Mrs. Watson closed the door and went to her bedroom. Paris finished up her last application, took a shower, and put on one of her sexy nighties. She felt better after talking to her mom and couldn't wait to go Christmas shopping. Thoughts of the interview raced through her mind. What should she wear? How should she do her hair? Should she get a manicure, a new suit, bag, shoes, etc.? One thing she knew for certain, she would have to get up early Monday to get her hair and nails done. She would be ready for Tuesday. With a smile on her face, Paris closed her eyes and whispered a sweet "thank you" to God for her family and the interview.

# Chapter 6

As Payton entered the senior living home, he was greeted with Christmas music and three female workers with gifts for him.

"Ladies, ladies, what is all this? The Christmas party hasn't even started yet."

"Yeah, we know!" yelled Angela. "We knew you were working for David tonight, and this is your last day this week, so here you go." Angela handed Payton his gifts and gave him a hug. "We wanted to show you how much we appreciate you working extra hours here, keeping us company, and making us laugh."

"Thank you so much, ladies."

Payton gave each lady a hug and a kiss on the cheek. He then signed in and checked the board to see whom he was assigned to. He noticed his name besides his usual Mr. Rhodes, whom he enjoyed sitting with. However, realizing he had to sit with Mr. Joyner was something new. Mr. Joyner insisted on having David and only David sit with him. No one at the senior living home knew why and didn't ask. But if David was at work, he was always requested by Mr. Joyner.

"Hey there, Mr. Rhodes. You ready for Christmas?"

"Yes, sir, my family will be here tomorrow to spend Christmas with me. How's your family?"

"Ahhh, we're doing good, doing good. So what would you like to do today? Play dominoes or cards?"

"I was thinking about playing some dominoes. You know, son, you haven't beat me yet, and I want to give you that chance before I kick the bucket."

"Mr. Rhodes, you know you ain't going nowhere. Plus, you gotta come to my championship game Sunday."

"On Christmas?"

"Yes, sir, we play tomorrow, party on Saturday, and win the championship on Sunday."

"Oh my, what is the world coming to? Playing games on Christmas. Christmas is a time to be with family and friends, enjoying each other, eating good food, drinking hot cocoa, and getting drunk."

"We're gonna do all that, Mr. Rhodes, except get drunk. My dad would kill me if he knew I was drinking at my age. My grandparents and cousins are coming in Saturday. Then I'm taking my cousins to a party. And Sunday, we're all going to church and then to my game. And then, Mr. Rhodes, after we kick butt and win the championship game, we're all going out to party all night long."

"Now that sounds like a plan, young man. But don't you think you party too much?"

Payton laughs. "Not at all. I'm young, sir. You should come to the game and see me play."

"I don't know, son, but I'll see. Sunday, right?"

"Yes, sir."

"What time?"

Payton replied, "5:00 p.m. sharp!"

"I can't promise you anything, but I'll see if my daughter can bring me."

"Fair enough, Mr. Rhodes. It's going to be an awesome game. So how is Lexi doing anyway?"

"She's fine, pregnant again. It's a girl this time, and she and Rick are delighted about that."

"That's nice, Mr. Rhodes. Please tell her I said hi when you see her, okay."

"Sure will, son. Now let's get on with the game before I fall asleep."

They laughed.

"Yes, sir."

Payton grabbed the box of dominoes off the bookshelf, and they played a nice, quiet game of dominoes.

"Well, Mr. Rhodes, looks like you beat me again. I just don't know how you win week after week."

"Young man, I got skills. You could learn a thing or two from me, ya know."

"Oh really. Well, can you tell me how to settle Mr. Joyner down? I gotta go see him now, but the only aide he wants in his room is David."

"Ahhh, good ole Mr. Joyner. He still on that biblical trip. He only asks for David because of his name. You know the story about David, right?"

"Yeah, a man after God's own heart."

"Sho' 'nuff. But Mr. Joyner doesn't know why David works here."

"That makes two of us."

Payton chuckles.

"Well, I'm not spilling the beans, but we all fall short of the glory of God."

"True that, Mr. Rhodes. It's all good. See you Sunday, old man."

"Old man? Who you calling old? I can…"

Payton ran out of the room laughing as Mr. Rhodes raised his fist in comical anger.

Payton made his way to the nurses' station to let them know that he was heading to Mr. Joyner's room. He was surprised to see only one nurse at the station, especially when there should always be two nurses at the nurses' station.

"Hey, Ms. Angela. Mr. Rhodes is good to go. I'm on my way to see Mr. Joyner."

"Got it. He's actually in good spirits today, so you'll probably be fine."

"What! It must be the Christmas aura. By the way, where's Rhaina and Mya?"

"Rhaina is putting the finishing touches on the party decor, and Mya's showing the new security guard around."

"What new security guard?"

"Oh yeah, I forgot to tell you. Officer Brown is the new security guard. Just started tonight, and he already tried to talk to me and

Rhaina. Ain't that some shit? He looks like he's full of bull, and I ain't got no time for that mess. Only silly ass Mya would fall for his bull-shit game. I can imagine 'how she's showing him around.'"

"What? She better chill. Isn't she married?"

"She doesn't care, her husband cheating too, so there that is! Bam!"

"Girl, you're a hot mess."

"Ain't I?" They laughed. "So you know Rhaina wants to do you, right?"

"Rhaina, what! She's like what…twenty-six? I'm seventeen. She's a bit too old for me."

"Well, you're right about that. But all I'm saying is she wants you…bad!"

"So where's your man at?"

"Please! I'm single and loving it. All I care about now is getting my little angel ready for kindergarten next year."

"Sweet, she's five already."

"Yep, turned five last month and grown as ever, but I be spanking that ass right back in check."

They laughed.

"I know that's right. Well, let me go see Mr. Joyner, and then I'll head down to the party."

"Okay, baby, see you later."

Payton made his way to Mr. Joyner's room but couldn't seem to remember where he heard Officer Brown's name. It bothered him that he couldn't remember. He began to think about Tiffany and wanted to call her, but then he realized that he didn't have her number. He couldn't believe that he didn't ask her for her number. He solemnly made his way to see Mr. Joyner.

"How are you doing tonight, Mr. Joyner?" asked Payton as he entered the room.

No response. Payton walked slowly toward Mr. Joyner's bed.

"I said, how are you doing, Mr. Joyner?"

"Oh, hey, David. I'm doing fine. How about you?"

"No, Mr. Joyner. I'm Payton. David is off tonight."

"Why?" Mr. Joyner asked as he opened his eyes.

"We switched shifts because I have—"

Mr. Joyner cut him off. "Oh, I see. Well, I don't need anything but some crackers and water. If you can get that for me and then go, that would be great."

"Sure thing, Mr. Joyner, sure thing. I will be right back."

Payton went downstairs to the kitchen to get the crackers and water. He could hear the music pumping from the recreation room and decided to peep in. The room was decorated nice, and the food looked delicious. A few of his coworkers were dancing and having a good time. Payton couldn't wait to join them. He turned around in a hurry and bumped into the security guard.

"Oh, excuse me," said Payton.

"No problem, son. Where are you rushing off to?"

Payton couldn't believe it. It was that officer again. *Why is he everywhere I am?* he thought to himself. *What is up with this dude?*

"Oh, hey, Officer…Brown, is it?"

"Yes, that's me."

"I'm heading back upstairs to see Mr. Joyner. So you work here too?"

"Yup! I do security here on my nights off."

"And at the school?"

"Yup! Brother gotta make that paper."

"True that. Well, I gotta go."

"Okay. Hurry back so you can join the party."

Payton didn't respond. He headed to the staircase, rushed up the stairs and to Mr. Joyner's room. When he entered, he heard Mr. Joyner snoring, so Payton quietly placed the crackers and water on the nightstand and exited the room. He rushed to the bathroom to call Garrett.

"Yo, G, you won't believe who works here."

"Who? That cutie you've been trying to get with."

"Nah, man, Officer Brown."

"Officer Brown?"

"Yes, the security guard from 8 Ball. Now don't you think this is getting weird? He seems to be everywhere I am. What's up with that? He better not be stalking me like some punk dude. I ain't with that shit."

"P, man, he's a security guard. I wouldn't worry about him."

"Yeah, maybe you're right."

"Well, did he say anything to you?"

"Not really."

"See, nothing to worry about."

"I'm not worried, man."

"Bro, I gotta go. Nikki giving me the eye."

"Okay, G, see you tomorrow."

Payton headed back downstairs and joined his coworkers at the party. He chatted and danced with a few of his coworkers before grabbing some food and joining Angela and Rhaina at the table.

"Hey, ladies, I'm back," he said as he sat down.

"Hey, handsome," said Rhaina. "Where have you been hiding your fine ass? Come over here and keep me company."

"I'm good, Ms. Rhaina. Thirty minutes to go, and I'm out."

"Boy, get over here and sit down. And my name is Rhaina. I don't know what that Ms. Rhaina crap is all about."

They all laughed, and Angela gave him that "you better watch out" look. Payton got up and went to sit next to Rhaina.

"I'm just trying to be respectful, Ms. Rhaina—I mean, Rhaina."

"Payton, do I look like an old lady to you?"

"No way, ma'am!"

"I don't think so either. So please call me Rhaina, okay?"

"Okay. So how's the family, Rhaina?"

"They still tripping over my brother. He goes back to court next week, like right after Christmas, so you know my parents are bugging out. They're praying he doesn't get thrown in jail."

"Why, what did he do now?"

"Stole some credit cards and went shopping for his two rug rats."

"What, he's bold as hell. Why would he do something like that? Wasn't he thinking about his kids?"

"We asked him the same thing. He says *that's why he did it.* He said his kids were going to have a good Christmas this year…no matter what. Don't make no sense to me 'cause now he's facing like ten years in the pen because he's on probation from that check fraud case. He keeps blaming it on the fact that he got laid off. I tried to get him the janitor job here, and he told me he ain't mopping no floors. Now ain't that some shit because that's just what he might end up doing. His stupid ass."

"Damn. He got some serious praying to do. I'm going to pray for him, Rhaina."

"Thanks, Payton. Oh yeah, Payton, that new security guard asked me some questions about you. I was like, what the hell he want to know about you for? I didn't disclose anything. I think he's a bit shady."

"What? You serious?"

"Yup. I just told him that we don't give out any personal information about the employees."

"I really appreciate that, Rhaina. Well, ladies, it's been real once again. I gotta go. See y'all next week," said Payton as he got up from the table.

"Wait, one minute!" yelled Rhaina as she stood up. "I didn't get my dance with you."

"Rhaina, I gotta go," said Payton with a smile. "I'm tired."

"Boy, you're too young to be tired. Get over here."

Payton was trapped. Rhaina grabbed his hands and led him to the dance floor. They danced and danced. Then she put her arms around Payton's neck and gave him that dirty eye look. She pulled him closer, grabbed his hands, and put his hands on her waist. He felt a bit uncomfortable, but at the same time, her soft hands on the nape of his neck felt really good.

"So, Payton, when are you coming over to my house?"

"For what?"

"What do you think? You have a girl?"

"Nah. I'm focusing on my academics this year."

"Oh, I see. Well, maybe you can focus on me too. What do you think?"

Payton blushed and couldn't believe this twenty-six-year-old lady was flirting with him. He thought she was cute and sexy as hell, but he also knew she was too old for him. His parents would not be happy if he brought a twenty-six-year old lady home, talking about that's his girlfriend. He smiled at the thought.

Rhaina moved in closer and whispered in his ear, "Boy, I can show you a few things and make you feel real good. I know you're a virgin, so I'll be gentle."

Payton gave her a surprising look and a handsome smirk. "Now how do you know that, Rhaina? I keep my personal business to myself. And don't you have a man?"

"Don't you worry about that," replied Rhaina. "Just know that I want to fuck you."

"Oh really?"

"Yup. And for the record, I dumped that no-job asshole. He was getting too needy, and I ain't got time for that. So when are you coming over?"

"Damn, girl. I just told you that I'm—"

Rhaina stopped him from speaking by putting her index finger on his lips. "Academics...sure."

"And that's the only thing on my mind."

"So you mean to tell me that you don't want none of this?"

"I didn't say that. I said—"

"Oh, I heard what you said. But you're not hearing me. I'm not looking for a relationship, Payton. I just want you to know that anytime, and I do mean anytime, that you need to relieve some stress or bust a nut, just let me know. We can keep this as casual as you like. Okay, handsome?"

Rhaina gave Payton a tight hug, slowly kissed him on the mouth, and left him on the dance floor. He turned around to watch her walk away, smiled, and shook his head. *I wouldn't even know what to do with that*, he thought to himself.

Payton headed to the employees lounge to gather his gifts and belongings. He couldn't wait to get in his Jeep to call Garrett. As Payton headed out of the building, he heard a voice. He turned around and to his surprise stood Officer Brown.

"Hi there, Mr. Watson."

"Oh, Officer Brown, hello."

"You're heading home, huh?"

"Yes, sir. Gotta go."

"Okay, well, get home safe. See you tomorrow night. And tell your mom I said hello."

Payton turned around and looked at the officer, kinda confused. He wondered why this man mentioned his mom. Payton was beginning to get anxious.

"Excuse me, Officer?"

"Tell Mrs. Watson I said hello."

"You know my mother?"

"Sure do," he replied quickly and went back inside the senior living home. Officer Brown stared at Payton as he locked the doors behind him. Then like a ghost, the officer disappeared.

Payton couldn't believe what just transpired. He began to get a bit suspicious because Officer Brown was showing up everywhere he seemed to be, and now the officer had the audacity to mention his mother. Payton rushed inside his Jeep and called Garrett.

"Yo, G, that officer told me to tell my mom's hi. What's up with that shit?"

"Man, I don't know, but I'm kinda busy right now."

"G, what's up with this guy?"

"Man, I'm busy…can't talk now. I'm at Nikki's chillin' and trying to get my early Christmas gift, and man, her parents ain't here either… Gotta go!"

"Say no more, man, later."

Garrett disconnected the call before Payton could respond.

Payton listened to the radio while he drove home. He couldn't get Officer Brown out of his head. He couldn't seem to shake the idea of this man mentioning his mother. Payton would definitely have to mention this strange encounter to his parents. Before he knew it, it was 11:00 p.m., and he was home. He thought of Tiffany again and wanted to text her but couldn't. He didn't have her number. But he knew he would see her at the game tomorrow and would find a way to get her number. Payton changed into a pair of shorts and jumped in bed.

# Chapter 7

Mrs. Watson was up early Friday morning, making breakfast for her family. She made her husband a cup of coffee and went upstairs to get ready for work. On her way, she stopped by Kennedy's room.

"Good morning, baby," she said as she opened the door. "Time to get up, Kennedy. You got thirty minutes."

"Okay, Mom."

When she returned to her room, Mr. Watson was sitting up in bed with his laptop.

"Good morning, baby," said Mrs. Watson as she leaned toward her husband and gave him a kiss on the lips. She put his cup of coffee down on the nightstand and sat in her favorite chair near the window.

"Good morning, sweetie. Are you going into the office today?"

"Yes, just for a little while. Kennedy and Paris are coming with me. We're gonna have lunch and then finish up our Christmas shopping. So you and Payton got the house to yourself. No crazy fun, got it. I made y'all some bacon, eggs, and grits."

"Got it, baby. Thanks for bringing my coffee up. I'm sure Payton will be resting up for his game tonight."

"I'm sure he will! Let me get dressed and get going. The earlier I get into the office, the sooner I'll be home, and we can all go to the game together. I'll bring home some Chinese food so we can eat before the game."

"Sounds like a plan, baby."

Mrs. Watson got dressed, kissed her husband goodbye, and went downstairs. Paris and Kennedy were in the kitchen, cleaning it up. When they were done, Mrs. Watson and her daughters got in her car and headed to her office.

"You're not working all day, right, Ma? asked Kennie.

"No, baby, just want to make sure the orders came in before the holidays, do some filing, and then we're going to lunch, then shopping!"

"Cool. Can we stop at Dunkin'? I need a croissant," said Paris.

"Girl, you just ate breakfast," said Kennie. "Are you eating for two?"

"Kennedy, please! You're obnoxious. Can you just be quiet and read your book?"

Mrs. Watson gave Paris a quick "you better not be" look. She knew Paris had a boyfriend, but she also prayed that her daughter would stay a virgin until she was married, like she did. Paris noticed the look on her mother's face and felt the need to calm her.

"Don't worry, Mom. I'm definitely not pregnant. Plus Derek and I are not seeing each other anymore."

"Oh, I didn't know that. Why didn't you tell me?"

"I tried to, but you and Dad have been so busy lately."

"True. Sorry about that. We can talk later, okay?"

"Really, Mom, it's okay. Leah has been helping me deal with it. Don't worry. Derek and I are still friends."

"Okay. But if you need to talk, I'm available."

"I know, Ma, I know."

As they waited on line at the Dunkin' drive-through, Paris figured this would be a good time to ask her mom about the argument she heard her parents having.

"So, Mom, the other day, I heard you and Dad arguing. What was all that about?"

"Oh, baby, nothing you need to be concerned with. He was a bit upset because he may have to travel next weekend."

"New Year's weekend?"

"Yup. And he's not too happy about it."

"Who would be? That's crazy. Grandpa could just close the office like he did this weekend."

"Yeah, I know, but two weekends in a row."

"Ah, so what. Who needs construction work during New Years?

"You know, Paris, you're right. And I'm gonna let Grandpa know exactly that on Christmas."

"Good idea, Mom, good idea."

When they got to the office, Mrs. Watson did some work online, made sure all her orders came in, and by twelve-thirty, they were off to lunch and Christmas shopping.

Payton rested at home most of the day. He wanted to be ready for tonight's game. He knew a lot was at stake. The winning team tonight plays the championship game on Sunday, and he wanted one of those teams to be his team. After Payton ate, he went upstairs to get dressed and headed to Garrett's house to pick him up.

*Beep! Beep!* "C'mon, man," Payton mumbled to himself as he waited for Garrett.

Payton wanted to get to the school early to warm up and give the team a pep talk.

"Sorry, man, Mom's bugging about the party tomorrow night."

"Why? She knows me."

"It's not you, P. She don't like that area too well."

"Ahhh, we'll be good."

"Yeah, that's what I told her."

Payton sped off to the game. They were at the school within minutes. They headed to the locker room to get into their workout gear. Soon, the rest of the team was in the locker room, changing too. Payton was surprised to see that Trey was on time and not high. Payton gave his teammates a good pep talk, and he could see that the team was ready and excited.

"Good to see you on time, Trey," said Payton.

"Man, shut up!"

"Damn, Trey, let up on ol' cappie!" said Alex.

"Whatever, man."

"So, P, man," said Garrett, "what the hell were you trying to tell me about that officer?"

"Man, he asked me about my mom's yo."

"What! He called you?"

"Nah, man. He ain't got my number. I ran into him as I was leaving work last night. Is that a coincidence or what?"

"Maybe not man."

"What do you mean?"

"When we hung up, I remembered something. Trey called me the other day, wanting to know where you worked."

"And you told him."

"I'm sorry, man. I wasn't even thinking—"

"It's okay, G. It's okay."

"But, P, I told Trey where you work, and all of a sudden, that officer shows up. That's odd. You gotta watch your back. Trey might be up to something."

"G, I'm really not worried about me. Officer Brown asking about my mom worries me. You can be sure that I'm going to find out what the heck is going on."

On the way to the gym, Payton saw the cheerleaders coming into the school. Payton eyes were fixed on Tiffany, and he knew he'd better get her number now because once he hits the court, it's all basketball.

"Yo, G, I'll meet you in the gym. I gotta see someone right quick."

"Okay, man, later."

Payton walked up to the girls, said hi, and then stepped to Tiffany. He thought she looked cute in her cheerleading sweat suit. He liked that she didn't overdo her makeup like some of the other girls do. He smiled and looked into her eyes as he stepped to her.

"Hey, Tiffany, how are you doing?"

"I'm good, and you?"

"I'm good. So you ready to cheer tonight?"

"I guess so," she replied shyly. "It's going to be crowded, and I think my dad is coming, and—"

"Girl, what are you worried about? You cheer really good, and I'm sure you know the routine. You'll be fine. Don't worry."

"Thanks for the confidence."

"No problem. So are you going to the party tomorrow night?

"I don't know. Shayla wants to go, but I'm not a hundred percent sure if I want to go."

"You should go…with Shayla, of course. She's cool."

"Yeah, she is."

"Well, if you change your mind, call me and let me know, and then I'll be able to keep you company while Shayla dances all night."

Tiffany chuckled.

"I guess, I can do that."

"Okay, put my number in your phone. It's 555-1228. Just let me know either way, okay? I gotta go now. See you later."

"Okay, cool."

Payton played like a pro. He felt really good too. He thought that maybe interacting with Tiffany before the game gave him that extra energy to play really well. Payton scores the winning points at the buzzer. They win. The crowd goes wild and rushes the court. All the cheerleaders ran to the team players and gave them hugs. A few of the cheerleaders hugged Payton and congratulated him on his win. By the time he made his way to Tiffany, she was smiling from ear to ear.

"What? No hug from the new girl?"

"Didn't you get enough hugs already?"

"Nope, I'm short one hug."

"You're spoiled!"

"Girl, come here and give me a hug. Tiffany stepped closer to Payton and gave him a quick hug. He barely had time to embrace the hug. He didn't want to let go but knew he had to. And he definitely didn't want to make it obvious that he was interested in her."

"Good game, Payton," she whispered in his ear.

"Thank you, Tiffany," he whispered back. "Maybe I'll see you later."

Just as Payton was disengaging from the quickest and sweetest hug he has ever had, he glanced toward the exit and saw Officer Brown who signaled him to come over. Payton stepped away and headed toward Officer Brown. He turned around and saw Tiffany walking toward the bleachers to a tall thick man waving at her. He thought that must be her dad and thought that it was nice that he came to watch her cheer.

"Another great game, son."

"Yeah, you can say that."

"I see your family came out to support you."

"You don't know my family."

"I know your mom, and from what I can see, she hasn't changed a bit."

"What do you mean she hasn't changed a bit? How do you know my mother?"

"We went to school together, and I used to—"

"You used to what?"

"It's not important. You best go get dressed so I can close up the school. But please tell your mom that Randy said hello."

"Yeah, sure. I'll tell her."

Payton ran toward the locker room. He felt a bit uneasy and wanted to know what Randy was talking about. Payton was just about to lose it and was getting tired of this man harassing him. He knew it was time to tell his mom and dad about the strange encounters with Officer Brown, and that's exactly what he did when he got home.

# *Chapter 8*

After the game, Payton and his friends headed over to his house to chill out. They played cards, checkers, pool, fools ball, and video games. Payton kept checking his phone to see if Tiffany had texted him about the party tomorrow. No texts or missed calls. Ughh.

"Dag, P, you checking your phone like every three minutes. We ain't never gonna finish this game."

"Man, shut up, I'm waiting on a text."

"From Tiffany," said Cameron in his girly voice.

"Nigga, mind your business." Payton put his phone in his pocket and continued to shoot pool.

Just then, Cameron's phone rang. It was his cousin Shayla.

"Hey, cuz, what y'all doing tonight?"

"We just chillin' at Payton's. What's up?"

"Nothing. We're bored."

"Y'all should come chill with us."

"Man, who are you inviting over to my house!" yelled Payton in the background.

"Tell Payton to be quiet. Nikki, Tiffany, and Desi are with me. Would that be okay?"

"Yo, P, can Shayla and her crew come over?"

"Is Tiffany with them?" asked Payton in a whispered voice.

"Yeah, man. So can they come over or what?"

"Man, I don't care. Just tell Shayla to park on the side of the house, near the garage."

"Hey, Shayla."

"Yeah, I'm here."

"P said c'mon. I'll text you his address and park near the garage."

"Boy, I know where he lives. See y'all in a few."

Payton knew that Shayla drove fast and would be at his house in a few minutes. He ran upstairs to freshen up. He was anxious and excited that Tiffany was coming over. On his way upstairs, he saw his parents in the kitchen getting the Christmas menu together.

"Hey, y'all."

"Hey, son. That was a hell of a game tonight."

"Thanks, Dad."

"You're ready for the big time, son. You know I got connections, right?"

"I've been meaning to talk to you and Mom about the whole pro thing. I want to wait on going pro. I really want to go to college and study to be a sports physician."

"Yeah, I know, but going pro is like money in the bag, son. You should really think about it."

"I will, Dad. By the way, Mom, do you know a Randy Brown? He stopped me after the game tonight and said he went to school with you and to tell you hi."

"Randy Brown? No, I don't recall the name. Is he a basketball coach?"

"No, he's a cop and a security guard at 8 Ball and at my job. He said he knows you. And he seems to be showing up everywhere I am. The games, 8 Ball, and my job. Don't you think that's kinda odd?"

"Yea, I do," said Mr. Watson as he gave his wife a questionable look.

"Baby, you just said he does security. So apparently, he's working security. I wouldn't worry."

"Okay, Mom. My friends are coming over to hang out for a little while. We'll stay downstairs and won't make too much noise."

"Okay, baby. But they can't stay here all night."

"I know, Ma."

Payton rushed upstairs, washed his face, brushed his teeth and hair, changed his clothes, and splashed on a bit of cologne. He wanted to look cool and smell good for Tiffany. He ran back downstairs and into the kitchen to get more sodas and junk food. As he was making his way down to the basement, he heard a horn beep. He figured it was Shayla, so he quickly dropped the goodies off downstairs and ran back upstairs to meet the girls in the driveway.

"Hey, ladies, how y'all doing?"

"We good," said Shayla as she exited the car. "Nice Christmas decor. Who did it?"

"The Watson Family Decorating Group."

"Hey, Payton," said Desi as she ran into the garage. "It's getting chilly out here."

Payton rushed to the back passenger side and opened the door for Tiffany. He couldn't wait to see her pretty face again. He hoped he could get at least two hours to spend with her. And he knew two hours would go by quick, so he planned to make the best of the time he had.

"You live here?"

"Yes."

"Well, it's beautiful, and the Christmas decorations out front are lovely. You guys do it up, huh?"

"My parents absolutely love Christmas."

"And what about you?"

"Actually, it's my favorite holiday."

"Mine too."

Payton led the ladies into the house and downstairs to the basement. Garrett and Cameron were playing air hockey. Alex was on the phone with Brie.

"That was quick," said Cameron.

"You know how I roll," said Shayla.

"You're gonna mess around and get a ticket," said Garrett.

"Boy, be quiet," replied Shayla. "The cops know me, and they sure ain't giving me no ticket. I'm too cute for tickets."

They all laughed.

"How you doing, Cam?" said Desi as she walked over to him and gave him a hug.

"I'm good Desi. How are you doing?"

"Great, now that I see you."

Cameron blushed and continued his game.

"Boy, stop being shy. We can chill together for the night. We're both single."

"Well, you're right about that. So what's up?"

They smiled at each other.

"Let's sit down and watch tee-vee," said Desi.

"Cool."

"Cam, man, we're not done playing!" yelled Garrett.

"You win, man, you win," said Cam as he walked off to watch television with Desi.

Cam grabbed Desi's hand and led her to the couch. He helped her take her coat off and sat down next to her. Payton led Tiffany to the plush love seat that only fit two people comfortably. He sat down next to her but not too close but close enough to talk privately.

"Do you want something to drink?"

"Sure, water will be fine."

"Be right back."

Tiffany took her coat off and got comfortable. She sent a text to her dad to let him know where she was, put her phone on vibrate, and tugged it away in her bag. She glanced over at Alex, and he was smiling from ear to ear. She figured he was having a really nice conversation with Brie. She noticed Desi staring at Cameron as he watched television. Shayla and Nikki were still chatting, and Garrett was leaning on the hockey game, waiting for Nikki to finish her chat with Shayla.

"Here you go, Tiffany."

"Thanks, Payton."

"You're welcome. See, I told you that you knew the routine."

"How do you know? You were in the locker room."

"Well, I saw half of the routine, and to me, it looked like you did your thing.

"Oh, you think so?"

"Yep, sure do."

"Well, thank you. And you played a really good game. That shot at the buzzer was awesome. Are you ready for the championship game Sunday?"

"Ready as I'll ever be. Most of my family will be there, so you know, I gotta represent."

"I hear ya."

"You cheering for the championship game, right?"

"As far as I know…"

"Cool. I bet Shayla got something really good planned for the half-time presentation."

"You talking about me, P?" yelled Shayla.

"Nah, girl, I was just telling Tiffany that I know you got something hot for half-time Sunday."

"You know it."

They all laughed. Nikki finished her chat with Shayla and walked over to Garrett to give him a hug. Shayla sat down on the barstool and played a game on her phone. Desi moved a little closer to Cam and whispered in his ear. Before long, he got up, grabbed her hand, and they headed to the bathroom. Payton moved a little closer to Tiffany and continued his conversation.

"So, Tiffany, have you decided about the party tomorrow night?"

"No, I haven't. That's Christmas Eve, and I really don't think my dad is going to let me hang out. We usually do something together on Christmas Eve."

"I can understand that. Well, if he has a change of heart, shoot me a text, and I'll come pick you up. You saved my number in your phone, right?"

"Sure did. And I will let you know."

"And since you're not sure, can I get a dance now?"

"You mean like right now?"

"Yeah, I wanna dance with you."

"Okay." Payton ran through his playlist and found one of his favorite slow songs. Then, without hesitation, tapped the repeat button. He didn't want the song to end. He dimmed the lights and grabbed Tiffany's hands. They slow danced. Garrett looked at Nikki with a smile and decided to slow dance too. Cam heard the music and exited the bathroom with Desi. He grabbed Desi by the waist and they slow danced.

"Well, I guess I'd better go sit in my car, huh?" said Shayla.

After a couple of repeated slow dances, it was time for Payton's friends to go. He didn't want the night to end, but he knew he needed to get some rest. Tiffany heard her phone buzzing and turned her head toward the couch. She turned back and looked into Payton's eyes and suddenly realized his eyes watched her every move. She wasn't sure if she should check her phone or not. And she definitely didn't want to return a stare. At that moment, she almost felt that she should tell Payton about Jarod.

"That's probably my dad," she said quietly.

"You gotta go?"

"Yeah, it's getting kinda late, and I don't want my dad to worry. He's good at that."

"Oh, okay. Well, I'm glad you came over. I had a really nice time."

"I did too, Payton. And thanks for having me over."

"Anytime!"

As Tiffany was about to go and check her phone, Payton leaned in to kiss her on the cheek. Tiffany saw it coming and slowly put her head down.

"What? I can't give you a kiss?"

"Payton," she replied slowly, "I have…to go."

They walked back to the couch. Tiffany opened her bag and took her phone out. She realized it wasn't her dad that texted her. It was Jarod, and he was going to be arriving tomorrow to spend the holidays with her and her dad. Payton saw the look on her face as if something was wrong.

"Is everything okay, Tiff?"

"Yeah, I just gotta go. Shayla, you ready?"

"Girl, I was ready when Payton played that damn slow music."

As they were gathering their things, they heard a loud snore. They all turned their heads to Alex who was knocked out with his phone to his ear. Cameron threw an empty water bottle at Alex, and he jumped up.

"Man, what are you doing?" Alex asked.

"Time to go, Alex. And you snore…loud."

"A'ight, cool. Let's go."

Alex was about to say good night to Brie but realized she had already hung up. Payton walked his friend's upstairs, said good night to his boys, and walked Tiffany to Shayla's car.

"Text me when you get home, okay?"

"Okay, Payton."

"Okay, good night. Shayla, no speeding."

Payton stood by the garage and watched Shayla's car drive out of sight. He had a great night. He won the game, his team advanced to the championship game, his family was arriving tomorrow, and he danced with a beautiful girl. *What could go wrong?* he thought. *This would be the best Christmas ever!*

# Chapter 9

Christmas music was playing throughout the Watson's house. Mrs. Watson's parents, sister, brother-in-law, and their twins were there. Mr. Watson's parents, brother, and sister-in-law, and their two kids were there too. Everyone was in a good festive mood. Family was moving all around the house, hugging and kissing one another as they were getting situated. The twins, Riley and Reagan, were laughing as they chased Kennedy around the house. Arianna was upstairs with Paris getting ready for the party. Nate was chilling with Payton in his room while he looked for something GQ to wear to the party just in case Tiffany showed up.

"Cuz, wait to you see Tiffany. She's gorgeous."

"Man, you said that about Val, and she wasn't all that."

"Cuz, that was like five years ago, and I was twelve."

"And?" They laughed. "Man, find something quick 'cause we gotta go. I gotta show you some new moves and meet the honeys."

"Whatever, Nate. You probably doing that same ole two step."

"Get outa here, cuz. So you got some friends to introduce me to?"

"Sure do. I think you'll like Shayla. She's mad cool, but she just got out of a relationship, so don't push, cuz."

"Thanks, cuz, I won't."

"Cool. Let's go eat. Food smells delicious."

Payton and Nate made their way to the kitchen to grab some food. Every Christmas Eve, the Watsons have a seafood feast: shrimp, lobster, crab cakes, salmon, mussels, shrimp scampi, crab legs, the works. Their whole family loved seafood, and everyone enjoyed eating it too. Paris and Arianna were already eating and pretty much waiting on Payton. Just then, the phone rang.

"Hello. Hello," said Mr. Watson. "Hello…"

"There it goes again," said Mr. Watson as he glanced at his wife. "That's the third time today, and yesterday, it happened twice."

"We're still getting crank calls, Dad?"

"Yeah, son, and when I find out who it is, I'm gonna—"

"Dad, it's Christmas."

Payton, Paris, and their cousins finished eating. They tidied themselves up, jumped in Payton's Jeep, and headed to the party. Payton checked his phone, no text from Tiffany, and no missed calls either. He hoped she would show up because he really wanted to see her and dance with her again.

"Oooh, I can't wait to get there," said Arianna.

"Cuz, you're gonna have mad fun. My best friend Leah is going to meet us there," said Paris.

"This party better be on point," said Nate.

"Cuz, I told you. It's gonna be on. We know how to party!"

"You're not picking up, Garrett?" asked Paris.

"Nah, he's riding with Alex and Cameron."

"Cool."

Within thirty minutes, they were at the party. Payton parked his jeep, and he and Nate helped the girls out. They got in line to enter the hall. Payton texted Garrett to let him know he was on line.

"G, we here. On line."

"Okay, man. We're inside already. Got two tables near the back."

"Cool. See you in a minute. Oh, is Shayla there? I want to introduce her to my cousin."

"Yeah, she here. Already on the dance floor."

"Okay. Cool. See you soon."

"My crew is already inside, and we got two tables, so when we get inside, just follow me."

"Got you, cuz," said Nate.

They paid their $5 and got their hands stamped as they entered the hall. Payton was smiling because soon, he knew he would see

Tiffany again. They made their way to the back of the hall. Payton introduced his cousins to his crew, Nikki, and Desi.

"Is Tiffany out there dancing with Shayla?"

"Nah, P, she ain't here."

"What?" Payton had an empty stare on his face as he looked at Garrett.

"She's not here, man," repeated Garrett.

"Damn. Well, cuz, you'll have to meet Tiffany later."

"No worries, cuz. Now which one of y'all is Shayla?"

"Dude, my cousin is over there, shaking her fat ass," said Cameron.

They laughed.

"Oh, my bad," said Nate. "Payton, go get Shayla so I can meet her."

"Be right back, y'all."

Payton made his way through the crowded dance floor to find Shayla. He made a pit stop at the men's room to check his phone in private. No text from Tiffany. As he made his way back to the table, he found Shayla on the dance floor with some dude. He quickly stepped to her as not to interrupt her groove.

"Hey, Shayla, how are you doing? Where's Tiffany?"

"I'm good," she said while she continued to dance. "I don't know where she is. I texted her, but she didn't respond."

"Oh, okay. Well, look. My cousin wants to meet you."

"Okay, Payton. I'll meet him in a bit."

"Cool."

Payton made his way back to the table alone, no Shayla and no Tiffany. He wondered what kind of night he was going to have. All he could think about was Tiffany and why she hadn't texted him or showed up at the party. He didn't think he would have a good night. Just then, Shayla arrived.

"Hey, y'all, what's up?"

"Not much," said Cam.

"Hey, Shayla, this is my cousin Nate. Nate, this is Shayla."

"Hi, Shayla, nice to meet you. Can I get you something to drink?" asked Nate.

"Sure, let's go," replied Shayla.

Nate and Shayla went to the soda bar to get something to drink. Not too long after that, Leah showed up. She and Paris hugged. Paris introduced Leah to Arianna, and the three girls headed to the dance floor. Garrett, Nikki, Cam, and Desi joined them. Alex and Payton were left at the table.

"Man, what's up?" asked Alex.

"Nothing, man. I just thought Tiffany would be here."

"Well, don't be a party pooper. You know how to have fun. And you don't need a girl to have a good time. So let's go ask those two cuties over there to dance because they have been staring at us for the last ten minutes."

"Man, you're right. Let's go."

Payton and Alex got up and walked over to the two cute girls. They asked the young ladies to dance. The girls obliged, and within minutes, they were on the dance floor having a good time.

"So, handsome, what's your name?" asked the cute girl.

"Payton. What's your name?"

"I'm Chloe."

"Hey, Chloe."

They danced and talked for a few minutes. Then Chloe excused herself and went to the restroom with her girlfriend. Payton and Alex made their way to the table. As they were about to sit down, Payton felt a tap on his shoulder.

"Hey, Payton, how are you doing?"

Payton knew that voice. It was Tiffany. He turned around with a big smile. His smile quickly faded when he saw a man standing behind her.

"I'm doing well, Tiffany. How are you?" he replied as he glanced over her shoulder.

"I'm good. This is Jarod. Jarod, this is my friend Payton, and this is Alex."

Jarod extended his hand to Alex for a handshake. When he reached out his hand to shake Payton's hand, Payton hesitated for a brief minute before he met Jarod's hand with a shake.

"We reserved these two booths, so sit wherever you like," said Alex.

"Thanks, man," replied Jarod. "Babe, you want something to drink?"

"Yes, thank you."

"Okay, I'll be right back."

Jarod went to get the drinks. Alex sat down to chill. Payton stepped a few feet away from the table and looked at Tiffany with a surprised look.

"Babe? Now I see why you've been hesitant and didn't text me last night or today for that matter."

"I wasn't sure how to tell you. And last night, the way you were staring at me, I wanted to tell you, but I—"

"Tiffany, it's okay. You don't owe me an explanation."

"I hope we can still be friends, Payton," said Tiffany as she gently placed her hand on his forearm.

"Sure, Tiffany, sure. Does he live here?"

"No, he's in town, visiting for the holiday."

"Oh, I see. He's staying with you…quite cozy!"

"Payton…"

"You know what, Tiffany, that's really none of my business. I'm sorry to pry."

Just then, Jarod returned to the table with the drinks. Shayla and Nate were right behind him with drinks too. Nate jumped in the seat next to Alex, and Shayla sat down next to Nate.

"Cuz," said Nate, "why are you looking so down? This party is on point."

"I'm good, cuz. Go dance or something."

"So you must be Jarod?" asked Shayla.

"Yes, I'm Jarod. Nice to meet you."

"Nice to meet you too," replied Shayla.

"Nate, this is Tiffany. Tiffany, this is my cousin Nate."

"Oh, you're Tiffany. My cousin said you were—who the hell!" Shayla kicked Nate under the table.

"Yes, I'm Tiffany. Nice to meet you, Nate."

"Same here. C'mon, Shayla, let me show you how we do it up north."

"Okay, let's go."

"C'mon, Tiffany, we might as well go dance too," said Jarod. "We can't be out here all night."

Payton watched as Jarod placed his hand on the small of Tiffany's back and led her to the dance floor. Alex looked at Payton, and he looked down right sad. All Alex could do was laugh. Payton didn't know what to do. He really just wanted to go home and rest up for church and the championship game. Thoughts started running through his head. He had hoped to have a really good time with Tiffany tonight. But that was not going to happen, not with Jarod hanging around.

"Man, cheer up. They don't even look good together."

"Nice try, Alex. They actually do look good together."

"You would say some stupid shit like that!"

"Well, I guess, I'll go find Chloe and have some fun."

"Now that's the spirit. Enjoy yourself, P."

Payton found Chloe at the soda bar and had a drink with her. They talked for a few minutes before Payton asked her to dance. A few fast songs were played then a slow jam. Payton looked at Chloe, and she looked at him and smiled. They embraced and started to slow dance to the music. Chloe felt soft and smelled nice, but Payton couldn't get Tiffany off his mind. He was not expecting her to come to the party with a guy, let alone her boyfriend. He thought he would have her to himself…all night.

"What's on your mind, Payton?"

"Not much."

"Something's on your mind, so you might as well spill it."

"Well, the championship game is tomorrow, and I want to win," he lied.

"You will. I've seen you play a few games, and y'all got it in the bag, so lighten up."

"I'll try."

"Can I help?"

"How?"

She nibbled on his earlobe, and when the slow dance was over, she grabbed his hand and led him out the back door.

"Where are we going?"

"To my car. I'm going to help you lighten up."

"Well…okay!"

Payton and Chloe jumped in the back seat of her car. Chloe sat on top of Payton and unbuttoned her shirt. She rubbed his curly hair, and as she closed her eyes, she kissed his ear, his cheek, and then his mouth. Payton returned the kiss and massaged Chloe's back and her butt. They opened their mouths and started tongue kissing. Thoughts of Tiffany ran through his mind, but he didn't want to ruin the moment, so he quickly let the thought of Tiffany escape his mind. Then what he fantasied Tiffany doing, Chloe did. She unbuttoned Payton's pants and pulled them down to his thighs, just enough to where she can reach his penis. As they continued to tongue kiss, Payton's nature started to rise. Chloe grabbed his penis and massaged it. Payton grabbed Chloe's breasts and massaged them with his hands. They both moaned and groaned as Payton got harder and harder.

"Suck my breasts, Payton."

"What?"

"Suck my breasts."

Payton undid Chloe's bra and grabbed her left breast. He licked her nipple with his tongue and then opened his mouth and did as she asked. Her breast tasted good to him, and he thought how good Tiffany's breast would taste. Chloe's breasts were nice and soft, and as Chloe's nipple got hard, Payton got harder. He continued to suck her breast and massage her butt. Then Chloe raised his head and tongue kissed him. She tenderly bit his bottom lip and kissed his neck. She opened his shirt and kissed his chest and licked his nipples. Payton was in heaven. He let her do as she pleased. He wanted to feel good tonight, and Chloe was making that happen. Chloe then moved slowly down to the floor and got on her knees. She grabbed his hard penis and kissed the head of it. Payton jerked.

"It's okay, Payton, relax. I know this ain't your first BJ."

"I'm just surprised is all." Payton was not about to tell a girl he just met that she would be his first BJ. He felt himself getting nervous and warm inside. He was getting anxious and felt the sweat beads growing on his forehead. Chloe felt his anxiety too and knew just how to make him relax.

"Just relax, Payton, and enjoy my work."

Payton tried to relax. He couldn't believe what was about to happen. He wasn't even sure he wanted it to happen. Her warm hands massaging his penis felt really good to him, and he didn't want her to stop. But he knew he wasn't fully engaged. Tiffany was on his mind. He couldn't concentrate. Then Chloe grabbed his penis again, kissed it, and opened her mouth to taste it.

"Chloe, hold up."

"Why? What's wrong?"

"Nothing. I just don't want to do this here…in a damn parking lot."

"Why not?"

"Because it's not the right place."

"Are you serious? It's mad dark, no one is out here, and I know you want me to."

"Chloe, get up…please!"

"Really?"

"Yes, really. Put your stuff on and let's go back inside."

"Wow, just like that, huh?

Payton didn't respond. Chloe fixed her clothes. Payton pulled his pants up and buttoned his shirt. They walked back into the hall, and as soon as he entered, he saw Tiffany staring in his direction. *Is she looking at me?* he thought. He hoped she wasn't staring at him and Chloe, but it really didn't matter anymore because she had a boyfriend.

"Chloe, it was nice meeting you and hanging out with you, but I gotta go. Can I call you later?"

"Sure. Let me put my number in your phone. Hope to see you later, Payton."

Payton headed to the table where his friends were sitting. Man, I'm about to head out. Ari, can you go get your brother? We gotta go to church in the AM, and I'm tired."

"Yo, P, who the hell was that hottie?" asked Garrett.

"That was Chloe."

"Who's Chloe?" asked Paris.

"Don't really know, just met her tonight."

"I saw y'all leave," said Alex. "Where'd y'all go?"

"To her car, man."

"Awww, shit," said Cam. "What did y'all do in her car?"

"None of your damn business, Cam."

They all laughed.

Arianna arrived back with Shayla and Nate. Two minutes later, Jarod and Tiffany were at the table, smiling from ear to ear. Payton couldn't stand it. Her smile was beautiful. Hell, she was beautiful, and he couldn't have her. Payton was ready to go. He started talking about the game as if that was really on his mind. How his Cougars were going to play a great game and win the championship. Tiffany's eyes were glued on him, and Jarod noticed it. He didn't know Payton, nor did Tiffany mention Payton to him, but Jarod noticed how Tiffany hung on to Payton's every word.

"Well, it was nice meeting you all," said Jarod, cutting Payton off. "We're gonna head out now. Good night."

"Hey, nice to meet you too, man. Good night, Tiffany, said Payton."

Tiffany waved goodbye as Jarod grabbed her hand, and they left.

"Yo Paris, who was that dude you were dancing with?" Nate asked. "Who was that dude you were dancing with?"

"Oh, that was Randy, and he sure can dance."

"Looked like he was doing more than dancing," added Leah. "And, girl, he looks old."

They laughed.

"Don't hate, Leah. He did feel nice, though. So nice I invited him over tomorrow."

"You did what?" shouted Payton. "You invited some stranger over to the house. Ma is gonna kill you, girl. You don't know anything about that dude."

"He's not a stranger, Payton. He said he knows you."

"Me? I don't know him."

"Yes, you do. He said he works at your job."

"What! You're talking about Officer Brown?"

"Yup, that's Randy."

"Paris, I don't think that was a good idea. Ma is gonna freak out."

"She'll be all right. You just wait and see. She loves Christmas and wouldn't mind at all."

"Yeah, right," said Payton. "Where's he at anyway?"

"I don't know. I think he left."

The crew exchanged good nights and left the party. Within minutes, they were home. Payton jumped in the shower. He couldn't sleep. He turned on his television but wasn't really watching it. He knew he had to get some sleep for it was now Christmas, and he had a championship game to win. But something bothered him. He felt defeated and a bit betrayed. But why he felt betrayed, he didn't have an answer for that. Tiffany didn't lie about Jarod. He never asked her if she had a boyfriend or not. But she had to know that Payton was attracted to her. Just as he turned off the television, his phone buzzed. It was a text…from Tiffany.

"Hey, Payton. It was nice seeing you tonight."

"It was nice seeing you too, Tiff."

"I see you met someone?"

"Nah, not really. Did you have a good time?"

"Yeah, but Jarod can't dance, LOL."

"LOL. You should have danced with me…"

"Jarod would not have liked that…"

"You're texting me, and your boyfriend is there with you?"

"He's sleeping. I just wanted to say sorry for not telling you about Jarod."

"Hey, no worries. You didn't have to offer that up. If I wanted to know, I could have asked you."

"Yeah, but I kinda felt that you were attracted to me, and I could have told you about Jarod…"

"Well, to be honest, you seem really cool, and I was hoping to get to know you better. I guess we can be friends…"

"Sounds good to me, Payton."

"Cool. Well, I got an early day tomorrow, Tiff. Merry Christmas and G'nite!"

"G'nite, Payton!"

# Chapter 10

Payton really enjoyed the Christmas holiday season and couldn't wait to get his game on. He was in for a busy day and knew that he would need a hefty breakfast and rest after church. Rest would do him well as he had one heck of a Saturday night.

He woke up thinking about Tiffany and wondered if Jarod slept in her room or not. He didn't know why that was on his mind, but the thought of Jarod spending the night with her, under the same roof, bothered him. He wanted to text her but thought against it.

He thought of Chloe too and how close he came to his very first BJ. What was he thinking? Chloe was ready, and he backed down. *She probably thinks I'm a punk*, he thought to himself. *I'm not going out like that*, he said to himself. He would make it a point to try to see her again. He figured he would text her.

> "Gm, Chloe. It was nice meeting you last night. Merry X-mas!"
>
> "Hey, Payton. Ditto. Merry X-mas to you too. I'll be at the game tonight!"
>
> "Cool. See you later."

Payton threw his phone down on his bed and jumped in the shower. As he made his way back to his bed, he gently kicked Nate who was sleeping on a blow-up bed nearby.

"Get up, cuz. Time to shower, eat, and get ready for church."

"I'm up, P. Let me know when you get out the shower."

"I just got out. Your turn."

Nate got up and jumped in the shower. Payton grabbed his Christmas suit out of the closet and laid it on the bed. He undid the towel around his waist and put on some shorts and a T-shirt. He splashed on some cologne and headed downstairs.

"Someone's mad happy this morning," said Mrs. Watson as she glanced at her son coming down the stairs.

"It's Christmas, Ma, everyone's happy."

"What time is your game tonight?"

He answered, "5:00 p.m., and all y'all better be there."

"We will, baby. Go on and make your grandparents' plate."

"Okay, Ma."

Soon, the Watson family was all gathered around the dining room table ready to eat breakfast. Mr. Watson said a lovely prayer, and after everyone said amen, they dug into their plates. Festive chatter was going on between the family, and everyone was enjoying the moment.

"Oh, Ma, Mr. Rhodes may come to the game tonight, so please be on the lookout for him. His daughter Lexi is visiting for the holidays. Text me if they show up, okay?"

"That's nice," said Mrs. Watson. "Okay, I will. It's a blessing to be around family on Christmas. Not too many people can say that these days. I'm so happy my family is here with me."

"Now, honey, don't go getting all teary-eyed on us," said Mr. Watson. "Let's eat this awesome breakfast you cooked and get to church."

After breakfast, everyone freshened up and got dressed for church. Paris, Nate, and Arianna rode with Payton. He had to leave earlier than usual because he was in the choir. Mr. and Mrs. Watson gathered the other family members in their cars, and they were on their way to Christmas service. When Payton reached the church, he stayed in the car to call Tiffany. He wasn't sure if he should call her or not, but he wanted to hear her voice. Paris and Arianna got out and went inside the church."

"Hi, Tiffany?"

"Yes. Hey, Payton. This is a nice surprise."

"So how is your Christmas so far?"

"So far, it's great. How's yours?"

"Not bad. My family is here, and that's enough for me."

"You mean to tell me that's all you wanted for Christmas?"

"Yup."

"I find that hard to believe." She chuckled.

"Ha, that's because you don't know me very well."

"I guess, I don't."

Payton laughed. "Well, enjoy your Christmas, Tiffany."

"You too, Payton, goodbye!"

Payton put his phone in his pocket and headed inside the church. Thoughts of Tiffany ran through is mind. He couldn't believe how his feelings were growing for her, knowing that she was with Jarod. He knew he had to shake it off. How could he get involved with any-one now? He was about to finish his senior year, and he didn't need any distractions…not any. And then he thought about Chloe. And she was going to be at the game tonight too.

"Cuz, that was a smooth move…to call her after what happened last night."

"Man, I can't even trip. I'm not surprised she has a boyfriend. She's beautiful."

"She sure is."

"Told ya!"

Payton entered the church and met up with his fellow choir members. They all shared hugs, kisses, and daps. Nate joined his family in the pew. Soon, the choir came out from the back singing a Christmas song as they made their way to the choir loft.

Pastor McNight preached a wonderful sermon on the love of Jesus Christ and that the spirit of Christmas is all about giving. And how God's love is unconditional. And how we should love our ene-mies how God loves us.

"And now, church," said Pastor McNight, "we will hear the final Christmas selection from our choir."

As the choir stood up to sing the final selection, Payton stepped to the mic. Grandma Watson was so surprised that she stood up and shouted, "That's my baby!" and lifted her hands. The congregation laughed happily as she sat back down. Payton sang an awesome rendition of "This Christmas" that brought his mom and grandmother to tears. At that very moment, Mrs. Waston was very proud of her only son. She felt blessed to have a son like Payton and thanked God for blessing her with a wonderful young man.

After Payton sang, Pastor McNight gave the benediction, and the choir made their way to the choir room. The congregation continued praising the Lord, thanking Him for His grace and mercy, and sharing Christmas greetings with the church members and their guests.

Payton made his way to his family and gave them all hugs. First his dad, then grandparents, cousins, sisters, and finally his mom. She gave Payton a tight lengthy hug. His mother wouldn't let go of him. She hung onto him as if he was leaving for the military.

"Ma, I can't breathe," said Payton. She clutched her arms around his body… She didn't want to let him go. "Ma," he repeated. "I can't breathe," he said with a slight laugh.

"Baby, you sang beautifully. I loved every bit of it."

"Thank you Ma. To God be the glory," said Payton.

Payton looked over his mother's shoulder and noticed Tiffany, Shayla, and Jarod sitting in a nearby pew. *Whoa*! he thought to himself, *I had no idea she would be at church today.* All the same, Payton was very happy to see Tiffany. He skillfully made his way over to her.

"Hi, Tiffany. Hey, Jarod. Nice to see y'all here," said Payton as he shared a hand shake with Jarod.

"Hey, Payton. Nice job up there," said Jarod.

"Thank you."

"You look surprised," said Tiffany.

"Nah, not really…just wasn't expecting to see you here…that's why I"—Payton saw the look on Jarod's face and decided not to say anything about the call—"well, never mind. Hey, Shayla," he continued as he and Shayla shared a hug and a kiss.

"What up, P!" She smirked. "Where's Nate?"

"Right over there."

"Oh, okay. I'm going to go say hi."

"I think he'll like that."

"Well, I have to agree with Jarod. That was a very nice performance, Payton. I didn't know you sing."

"Yeah, I can blow a little."

They laughed.

Payton started to feel a bit uncomfortable and really didn't have anything else to say, especially with Jarod standing there with them. What he really wanted to do, he couldn't. Tiffany looked like an angel in her winter white dress. All Payton wanted to do was hug and kiss her, touch her hand, and tell her how lovely she looked. It was hard for him to restrain himself, but he knew he had to.

"We better get going Tiffany," said Jarod as he put on his coat.

"Okay, Jarod. I'm ready."

\*\*\*\*\*

Jarod picked up Tiffany's coat from the pew and helped her put it on. He felt a bit uneasy as well and just wanted to get out of there. He had already witnessed Tiffany's face light up when Payton approached them. And he couldn't help but notice how Tiffany didn't take her eyes off Payton as he performed a solo. Jarod figured his only escape was to remove Tiffany from Payton's presence…so it was time to go.

"Enjoy the rest of your holiday, Payton," said Tiffany as Jarod put his arm over her shoulders. Jarod needed Payton to know that Tiffany was his.

"You too, Tiff. See you at the game tonight."

Tiffany, Jarod, and Shayla headed to the double doors that lead to the lobby of the church. And right before they exited, Jarod planted a kiss on Tiffany's cheek. Jarod knew Payton was watching, and he wanted to make sure Payton saw the kiss to emphasize even more that Tiffany was his girl. Then as Jarod opened the door to the lobby, Tiffany turned her head around and smiled at Payton. He returned a bleak smile.

\*\*\*\*\*

Payton joined his family and realized his mom was staring at him. He tried to put on a happy face but failed. He hoped his mom didn't see the interaction with Tiffany and Jarod because for him, it was quite embarrassing.

"Hey, baby, who were you talking to?"

"Oh, that was Tiffany and Jarod."

"Friends of yours?"

"Tiffany is. I don't know Jarod."

"Well, I saw how she was looking at you, and I can tell you one thing…she adores you."

"Ma, please."

"And from the look on your face, I'd say that you adore her too."

"Mom, we're just friends," he said with a smile.

"Well, it's Christmas. So what she has a boyfriend. She also has a great friend in you, and I think she really appreciates that."

"Thanks, Mom."

*****

## Christmas dinner

The Watsons enjoyed a delicious Christmas dinner with their family. Payton ate light as not to be too full for the game. After Payton ate, he headed upstairs to rest. As he made his way to the staircase, he heard the doorbell ring.

"I got it!" yelled Paris as she ran from the formal living room.

Payton stopped halfway up the staircase to see who it was. He remembered that Paris had invited Randy over for dinner. Paris opened the door and put her hands on her hips.

"You made it!" she said as she opened the door.

"Yup. I told you I was going to stop by."

"Well, come on in out of the cold and meet my family. We're all chilling in the living room."

"After you," he replied.

Payton's jaw dropped as Paris's guest stepped into his parents' house. He thought he was going to fall out. He couldn't believe his eyes. This guy is bold as hell. Payton wanted to run down the stairs and get this creep away from his family. But before he could move, Randy was taking off his coat and following Paris into the living room. And as Randy followed Paris, he looked in Payton's direction and winked at him.

*What the fuck*! thought Payton. *This nigga here, at my house, trying anyway he can to get to my mother.* Payton had to do something.

"Yo, Paris, Paris, Paris…"

Paris ignored Payton, grabbed Randy's hand, and led him to the living room.

"Family, I have someone for y'all to meet. Her family stopped what they were doing and looked in her direction."

Payton was still on the stairs, wondering what the hell just happened. He rushed down the stairs and toward the living room. Payton stood on the steps that led down to the living room.

"Ma, Dad, family, this is Randy."

Everyone had empty looks on their faces because no one but Payton and Paris had ever seen this man before. Then Payton glanced over to his mother and saw that "look" on her face. It was a frightened look, an uneasy look. He knew right then that she knew Randy. Mr. Watson noticed his wife nervously pick up a few empty dessert plates and head toward the kitchen.

"You all right, baby?" asked Mr. Watson.

"Yes, honey, I'm just gonna get these dishes out of the way."

"Let me help you, Ma," said Payton.

Payton and his mother made their way to the kitchen. Payton noticed his mom was still shaking, and he wanted to console her. He took the dishes out of her hands.

"So, Ma, from the looks of it, you know this dude," said Payton as he put the dishes on the counter.

"Payton, you don't need to be concerned. Go upstairs and get some rest. You got a game in a few hours."

"Ma, I'm not going anywhere until I know that you're okay."

"I'm okay, baby, now go upstairs and rest."

"Ma, I'm not going…"

"Payton, please!" yelled his mom.

Payton saw a tear roll down his mother's cheek. He stepped closer to his mom and gave her a hug. Just then, Mr. Watson stepped into the kitchen.

"Payton, go upstairs!" yelled his father.

Payton turned around and saw his dad standing near the kitchen entrance.

"Okay, Dad. I don't know what's going on, but that's the guy that's been at every one of my games, 8 Ball, and my job. That's the guy that said he knows you, mom, and now he's here with Paris. What's up with that?"

"Payton! Upstairs…now!" shouted his father.

Payton put a pep in his step and headed up the rear staircase. He stopped midway up the stairs to hear what his parents were talking about. He wanted to know what the hell was going on. Payton saw the hurt in his mother's face and heard the annoyance in his father's voice. And he did not like any of it.

Mrs. Watson couldn't look her husband in the face. Ashamed and not sure what to do, Mrs. Watson slowly walked toward the sun-room and sat down on the couch. Mr. Watson sat down next to her and rubbed her back. Then Payton heard something he didn't want to hear.

"So, baby, it seems to me that you know this guy."

Mrs. Watson didn't answer.

"Sweetie, you're clearly uncomfortable with this Randy guy being here. We're not going to get into a deep conversation about it right now because it's Christmas and family is here. But we *will* talk about this later."

"I think I know him, and I think he's been crank calling the house."

"Are you sure?"

"Pretty sure."

"Well then, that's that. I'm going to tell him to leave. Go upstairs, baby, and lay down. We'll finish this conversation later."

Mrs. Watson got up and headed upstairs. She cried softly as she headed to her bedroom. She realized her secret was about to unfold right before her eyes. She knew that she would have to explain Randy's unexpected presence to her husband soon. She was hoping that time would never come.

Payton was fuming as he ran up the stairs before his mother could see him. He needed to hear no more. When he got upstairs to his room, he called Garrett.

"Yo, G. You're not gonna believe this bullshit."

"What's up, man?"

"That officer, Officer Brown, he's here with Paris, and my mom says she's pretty sure he's the one that has been crank calling the house."

"Yo, P, that's messed up. What you wanna do?"

"Nothing yet, G. I'll find him after the game and get to the bottom of this. See you later, man."

"Okay. You know I got your back, man."

# Chapter 11

The Watson family jumped in their cars and headed to the game. Mr. Watson couldn't wait to see his son do his thing. As good as a player he was, Mrs. Watson prayed that Payton and the team would have a great game and that her son would be selected as the most valuable player.

And with one second to spare, Payton threw up a three-pointer. He didn't make the shot. The crowd sighed. The referee blew his whistle. Payton was fouled by a player from the opposing team. The crowd cheered as Coach Monroe called his final time-out. Everyone stood up. The coach from the other team was arguing with the referee on the call because his team was up by two points. The foul stood, and as Payton and his teammates made their way back on the court, the crowd started clapping and yelling, "Go, Cougars, go! Go, Cougars, go! Go, Cougars, go!"

Payton made his way to the foul line, prayed and successfully made all three shots. The Cougars were up by one point. With one second to go, the Panthers had the ball and needed to take a shot. Number 12 threw a long pass to number 4 at the other end of the court. The Cougars were in place to defend. Number 4 threw the ball up in the air as soon as it reached his hands. Everyone was quiet. The ball hit the backboard and bounced off the rim. And then the twenty-four-second clock buzzed. The game was over. All the Cougars ran to center court, jumping up and down and high-fiving each other. The Cougar fans jumped for joy and made their way to the court. The cheerleaders ran to the players to congratulate them. The Cougars and Panthers exchanged "good game" daps and went to their assigned seats to await the announcement of the MVPs. When the center court was a bit cleared, the commentator stepped up to the mic to make an announcement. As Mrs. Watson prayed, she heard the announcer say, "And most valuable player for the Cougars is Mr. Payton Watson." The crowd on the court started yelling and clapping their hands as Payton got up from his seat and walked to center court to receive his MVP trophy.

Payton was tired and very happy at the same time. He didn't get much rest and was a bit off on his game. Payton didn't like that Randy upset his mother, and he wanted to talk to Randy right after the game. Payton looked around for Tiffany, but there were so many people on the court celebrating that he couldn't find her. As he celebrated, he felt a tug on his jersey. He turned around. It was Tiffany, smiling her beautiful smile at him. Payton thought how lucky Jarod was to have her. She was simply beautiful.

"Hey, Payton," said Tiffany as she gave him a hug. "Great game, and congratulations on winning MVP! That's awesome! I'm so happy for you."

"Whoa. What's up with the big hug? Jarod might see this…"

"Oh, he won't. He's not here."

Payton looked at Tiffany in an odd way. He wasn't sure he heard her correctly, and he definitely wanted to be sure he did.

"Excuse me," he said.

"Jarod's not here, Payton. He left a few hours ago," she continued as she stared into Payton's eyes.

"Really!"

"Yes, really. I'll fill you in later. Right now, go enjoy your championship."

Payton rejoined his team and the celebration. He saw Randy in the distance, controlling the crowd, and figured he would wait to talk to Randy at 8 ball. Then someone tapped him on his shoulder. He turned around, and Chloe had a big smile on her face.

"What a game, man. You can really play."

"Thank you, Chloe."

"Was that your girlfriend?"

"Nah, just a friend."

"Oh, cool because I'm feeling you, and I hope we can continue where we left off."

"I gotta go, Chloe."

"Okay. See you later, I hope."

The team ran to the locker room, showered, and changed their clothes. Payton's phone rang as he exited the locker room.

"Hey, Mom, how are you doing?"

"I'm fine. Just wanted to say congratulations on winning the championship and getting MVP. I'm so proud of you. I was trying to get to you before you headed to the locker rooms, but you guys were overtaken by the spectators. I didn't see Mr. Rhodes in the crowd. Plus it was way too many people in there. Do you think he made it to the game?"

"I doubt it. I'll try to stop by to see him tomorrow and give him the good news."

"Okay, baby. I'm sure y'all are going out to party. Your cousins are going to the party with Paris. Please look after them, Payton. Have fun and be safe. I'll see y'all later."

"Okay, Mom. Thanks. Love you."

"Love you too!"

Payton and his crew headed to the celebration party.

As the team entered 8 Ball, they were jumping and yelling, "We're number one! We're number one!" The energy at 8 Ball was so high. The whole team was there, the coaches, the cheerleaders, his cousins, friends, and even the Panthers. Payton was feeling happy again. He was excited to have won the MVP trophy and appreciated his friends being happy for him. He and his friends found their favorite booth, and Payton placed his trophy on the table.

"Boys, this trophy is for y'all. We did this as a team, and I appreciate all your hard work, focus, and dedication. Great game, guys!"

"You're welcome, Cappie," they yelled back.

"Now let's party and have a good time!"

Payton couldn't wait to get his fun on. He waited a long time for this championship night, and now that it was finally here, he was going to enjoy it. Payton and his boys were chillin' at the table when Trey and his crew arrived.

"Yo, cappie, good game, but to be honest, you were a little off your game tonight. I don't know who decides on MVP, but my cuz should have won MVP, and you know it!"

"Yeah, you're right, Trey," said Damien.

"Whatever, Trey," said Payton.

"Yeah, whatever, man," said Trey as he walked away with his friends.

Yo P, don't pay him any mind. I'm happy for you. You deserve it man.

"Thanks, G, I really appreciate that. Your cousin is something else."

Payton and his friends starting digging into the pizza and the popcorn. They played a great game, and now they could eat like they wanted to. Payton was just about to bite into his second slice when he felt a warm hand on his shoulder. He looked up with a smile, hoping it was Tiffany.

"Hey there, handsome. I figured you and your crew would be here."

"Keisha? What are you doing here? You're back early," Payton said as he put the pizza down.

"Yeah, it's me. Surprise! My little sister got sick, so we had to come home sooner than expected. Why you look like you've seen a ghost? Aren't you happy to see me?"

"It's good to see you, Keisha."

"You didn't answer my question."

"Look, Keisha, I'm chillin' here with my boys, so I'm not going to play that game with you tonight."

"Whatever, boy, move over."

Keisha moved Payton over so she could sit down. Payton's friends were in shock and stopped eating their pizza. They were waiting to see what Payton was going to do next. Payton was surprised as well. He didn't expect to see Keisha until school started again in January, but here she was, in the flesh. Keisha grabbed a slice of pizza off the tray and took a bite. Just then, Shayla and her girls came over to the table. They all looked beautiful in their outfits, and they were ready to have a good time too.

"Hey, y'all, what's up?" said Shayla.

"Hey, cuz, said Cameron. Y'all just getting here."

"Yup, and we're ready to party."

"Hey, Shayla, how are you doing?"

"Oh, hey, Keisha. Welcome back. I thought you were out of town."

"Long story, girl, long story. This pizza sure is good."

"Well, we're gonna go mingle and have some fun. See y'all later."

All the fellas yelled back "later," except Payton. His eyes were glued on Tiffany, and her eyes were glued on him. She looked beautiful in her red sweater and black leather pants. Payton wanted to say hi and offer her a seat, but Keisha was in his way. Payton was waiting for Tiffany to get to 8 Ball, and now that she was there, he couldn't even get to her. All he could do was watch her walk away. He started to think that his night would be a repeat of the previous night, and he wasn't having that.

"Excuse me, Keisha, I gotta go to the restroom."

"Hurry up, Payton, so we can get on the dance floor."

Payton ignored her and went to find Tiffany. After a few minutes of searching, Chloe stepped in front of him.

"Hey, Payton, how are you doing?"

"I'm good. How are you?"

"Good now. Wanna dance?"

"Not right now. I'm looking for someone."

"That cheerleader?"

"Actually, yes."

"Well, I'm not one to stand in anyone's way. You have my number. I guess, I'll see you around."

"See you later Chloe," said Payton as he walked away.

A few minutes later, Payton found Tiffany dancing with Shayla and her crew. He walked up to Tiffany and whispered in her ear.

"Can we go somewhere and talk?"

Tiffany nodded.

Payton grabber her hand and led her to a corner in the game room. He wasn't sure what he was going to say, but he knew he had to say something.

"You look beautiful tonight, Tiffany."

"Thanks, Payton. So I see she's back."

"Yea. She just showed up and made herself comfortable as if we were still—"

"Together! I get it."

"No, Tiff. We broke up last year. And I have no plans to get back with her."

"So she just shows up on Christmas night, and nothing's up? That's hard for me to believe."

"Well," said Payton as he moved in closer to Tiffany, "I'm telling you, nothing is up with me and Keisha."

"Payton, look. She's obviously still feeling you, and I don't want to get in the middle of whatever it is y'all got going on."

Tiffany stepped back and turned to walk away. She knew now that what she had to tell Payton was irrelevant. There was no longer a need to fill him in on anything. But Payton was not about to let her get away, not this time. He knew Jarod wasn't around, so he had to make his move…quick. Payton gently grabbed Tiffany's arm and turned her around.

"Tiffany, Keisha and I are through. I swear. I'm over her, and she has to get over me."

"Yeah, well, apparently she hasn't."

"I can't control that, Tiff. I've told her time and time again that we are done. She'll eventually get the message. And I don't want you worrying about her. Just know that I am *not* with her anymore. Now didn't you have something to tell me?"

"Yea, but it's irrelevant now."

"Why is that?"

"Because of—"

"Tiffany," said Payton as he moved closer to her. "Didn't you just hear what I said? There's no Keisha, plus I have feelings for someone else, and I want to get to know her better."

Payton lifted Tiffany's chin and looked into her eyes. All he wanted to do was kiss her. Her lips looked so soft, and he wanted to taste them.

"I will tell you all about her as soon as you fill me in."

"Oh, you got jokes now," she said.

"Nah"—he smiled—"just fill me in."

"Well, you know Jarod left early, right?"

"Yup, you told me that."

"But I didn't tell you why."

"I'm listening."

"Jarod left early because of you Payton."

"What! What did I do?"

"Enough! Jarod said that he noticed the way you looked at me, and he later observed the way I reacted around you."

"Oh really? And how's that?"

"It's hard to explain, Payton, but I know that I like being around you. I hardly know you, and yet I feel something pulling me toward you, like I need to be around you."

Payton's face lit up. He was ecstatic. He smiled from ear to ear. He pulled Tiffany closer to him, looked straight into her eyes, and softly rubbed her hair. Then Payton sang a line from Jodeci's "Come and Talk to Me," "You look so sexy, you really turn me on, blows my mind every time I see your face, girl. May I kiss you?"

"Yes," she quietly responded.

Payton leaned in to give Tiffany a kiss. He was right. Her lips were soft as a pillow, and they tasted lovely. Tiffany kissed him back. He opened his mouth, and she opened her mouth. Payton put his tongue in her mouth, and Tiffany returned the gesture and put her tongue in his mouth. They passionately tongue kissed. Payton enjoyed every minute of it and didn't want it to end. But he had some follow-up questions.

"Can we get to know each other better, Tiffany? Would that be okay?"

"What about the rest of your senior year? You said you wanted to focus on your academics."

"You let me worry about that. People make time for things that are important to them."

They smiled at each other.

Payton hugged and kissed Tiffany again. Then they played a few video games before they went back to their friends. On their way back, Payton spotted Officer Brown near the front entrance. He was talking to some dude, but Payton couldn't make out who it was.

"Hey, Tiff, I see someone I need to talk to. I'll meet you back at the table, and I want an answer to my question, girl," he continued as he walked away with a smile on his face.

"Okay. See you later."

Tiffany headed to the table, and Payton made his way to the front door. By the time Payton reached the door, Officer Brown was alone and texting on his phone.

"Excuse me, Officer Brown."

"Yeah, what's up?"

"Can I talk to you for a minute?"

"Sure, man, what's up?"

"Man to man. I didn't appreciate you visiting my house earlier today and upsetting my mom. That wasn't cool."

"I had no intentions of upsetting your mom. Like I told you, I know your mom, and I need to give her something."

"She doesn't need anything from you. And why are you asking people about me? If there's something you want to know about me, you could have asked me."

"Oh, so you're big and bad now?"

"Excuse me?"

"Look, young man. Go enjoy yourself. I'll catch up with your mom sooner or later."

"Leave my mother alone, man. You got some hidden agenda or something? Why are you always around me and my friends? And my job? What's up with you, man?"

"Well, a man's gotta work to take care of his family."

"Whatever! I'm only gonna say this once. Stay away from me, my sister, and especially my mother. You got that!"

"Do you realize that you just threatened an officer, young man?"

"Call it what you want. I'm just telling you to stay away from me and my family."

"Why don't we take this outside?" said Officer Brown.

"We don't need to go anywhere. I've said what I had to say."

As Payton turned around to head back to his friends, Officer Brown grabbed Payton's arm. Payton jerked Officer Brown's tight grip off him and accidently hit the officer in the chin. Officer Brown then grabbed the back of Payton's shirt and led him out of 8 Ball.

"What the hell are you doing, man!" yelled Payton.

A few patrons near the entrance stopped and looked in their direction. They weren't quite sure if Payton was getting arrested or not.

"Calm down, Payton. I'm taking you outside to cool off."

"I don't need to cool off, man. I need you to get up off me."

"I have something to tell you. Shut up and listen."

They made it outside, and the officer led Payton to his car. Officer Brown held the passenger door open for Payton to get inside. The officer then ran around to the driver's side and hopped in.

"So what do you have to tell me?"

"I really wanted to speak to your mom about this first, but it seems like that won't happen."

"Speak to my mom about what?"

Officer Brown started his car and turned on the heat. Payton just wanted to get out of the car but was also a bit curious to know what the officer was talking about. Payton figured he would just be a few minutes.

"You see that envelope back there? Grab it for me."

"What's this?"

Officer Brown was silent. He watched as Payton read the address on the envelope, "Court of Child Welfare" Paternity Division. Payton wasn't sure why Officer Brown was showing him an envelope from the courts.

"Man, what the hell is this?" asked Payton.

"In that envelope are the results of my paternity test."

"And why the hell are you sharing this with me."

"Because…"

"Because what?"

"Because I'm your father!"

Payton couldn't contain himself. He was livid. "What the fuck do you mean you're my father? That's bullshit, man. I'm not even entertaining this nonsense. I'm out."

Payton reached for the door handle. Officer Brown clicked the auto-lock button.

"Let me out of this damn car, man."

"Payton, we need to talk."

"I have nothing more to say to you. Please let me out of the car, Officer."

Officer Brown ignored Payton's request and sped off.

"Where are we going?" asked Payton.

"To your house so we can show your mother the results."

"Didn't I just tell you to leave my family alone? You don't listen too well, do you?"

"Your parents must know the truth."

"What truth? All you spitting out is some bull. Stop the car, please, and let me out."

The officer ignored Payton and kept driving. Payton couldn't believe it. He was being taken against his will. Kidnapped by a psycho—what kind of mess is this. Payton knew he had to do something because he didn't know what this man was capable of doing.

"Your mother and I had an affair about seventeen years ago."

"I don't want to hear anything you have to say. Stop this car and let me out."

"We had a nice thing going because your dad wasn't always home. I guess, he had a feeling something was up because after a few months or so, he was home all the time. Your mom stopped calling and texting me. She wouldn't return my calls or texts. Then about five months later, I bumped into Jessica and noticed she was pregnant. I asked her if it was mine, and she said no, but the look on her face told me everything I needed to know…that she was carrying my child!"

"Can you please shut up. I don't want to hear your lies."

"I'm not lying, son."

"I'm not your son."

"We'll see. We are going to see the results together! This is a family matter, so we will see the results as a family!"

"You're crazy, man."

Payton noticed that Officer Brown was about to get on the highway. He quickly reached into his pocket and grabbed his cell phone to call his father. When Officer Brown saw this, he reached for

Payton's phone and jerked the wheel. Payton moved his hand away from Officer Brown, and the phone fell on the floor. Payton took off his seat belt and reached down to get his phone, but the officer stopped him. Officer Brown put his arm out and pushed Payton back into the seat. Payton pushed the officer's arm off him, which made the car enter the next lane. The officer attempted to get back into his lane but overcorrected. The car slid on the black ice and went through the guardrail, down an embankment, and crashed into a tree. Payton's body went through the windshield and landed on the hood of the car. Officer Brown's body smashed into the steering wheel. The car's engine died.

# Chapter 12

Payton's cousins and friends were having a great time at 8 Ball. Everyone was dancing, eating, and enjoying the music. After Paris and Leah finished dancing, they went to sit down to rest their feet. Arianna and Tiffany were sitting down, talking to Garrett and Alex. Nate and Shayla were having a great time dancing together. Cameron and Desi were chilling in the arcade.

"Hey, y'all, where's Payton?" asked Paris.

"Oh, he went to talk to some guy out near the soda bar."

"I'll be right back, y'all."

Paris got up and went to the soda bar. She saw a few of Payton's friends from school and kindly waved hello as she made her way to the soda bar. She knew one of the bartenders from high school and stopped to talk to him.

"Hey, Chase, how are you doing?"

"I'm good, Paris. How have you been?"

"Good. Still looking for a good-paying job, though."

"Aren't we all? You know, you can always work here."

"Thanks, but no thanks. Have you seen Payton?"

"Yeah. A few minutes ago. He was talking to the security guard, and then things seemed to get a little heated, and security took him outside."

"What? When? And what do you mean by heated?"

"Well, it looked like they were in a deep conversation, and then all I saw were hands and arms go up in the air. Then the security guard took your brother outside."

"Oh my goodness! I hope he didn't get arrested. Thanks, Chase. See you later."

"Later, beautiful! Call me, girl."

Paris went outside to see if she could find Payton. Payton was nowhere to be found. *Security guard*, she thought. *Chase couldn't have been talking about Randy. If Randy was here, he sure would have told me*, she thought. *Where are you, Payton?* she whispered to herself. Paris went back inside 8 Ball and rushed to the table.

"Garrett, did Payton call or text you?"

"Nah, why? What's up?"

"I don't know. Chase said he saw the security guard take Payton outside. I just went out there and didn't see either one of them. I think he got arrested."

"Hold up! What do you mean arrested? That's crazy." Garrett checked his phone. "No missed call or text from Payton. I'm sending him a text. He'll come right back like he always does."

"Did anyone else get a call or text from Payton?"

They checked their phones.

"Nope," they all said in unison.

Paris started to get worried and anxious. She couldn't imagine Payton getting into trouble with anyone, let alone the security guard. She decided to go find Nate to tell him the news and go home. Before she could take a step, Nate and Shayla showed up.

"Hey, cuz, what's up? You look bothered."

"I can't find Payton, Nate. And I think he got arrested."

"I doubt that. I'm sure he's fine. He may be taking a leak. I'll go check." Nate ran to the men's room to see if Payton was in there.

Alex joined him.

"Payton's been gone for a while now," said Tiffany. "Let me call him." Tiffany called Payton. "I got his voicemail, Paris."

"No text back yet, Paris," said Garrett.

"That's it," said Paris. "I'm calling my dad."

Paris moved to a quieter spot and called her father. She wasn't sure what she was going to say, but she had to tell him something. She prayed that she would stay calm.

"Hey, Dad."

"What's up, baby? Y'all having a good time?"

"Well, yeah, but I can't find Payton. Garrett sent him a text a few minutes ago, and he hasn't responded yet. Tiffany called him and got his voicemail. And I'm starting to get worried, Dad."

"Don't worry, baby. I'm sure he's fine."

"Dad?"

"Yes, sweetie."

"I think Payton was arrested."

"What do you mean arrested?" He sounded annoyed.

"I'm not sure what happened, but Chase said he saw the security guard take Payton outside."

"What security guard?"

"I don't know dad, but Payton's been gone for a while now, and I don't want to head home without knowing he's okay."

"Baby, you and your cousins come on home. I'm going to call the police station."

"Okay, Dad. See you later."

"See you later, baby."

Paris hung up with her dad. She was ready to go, but she worried about Payton. This was not like him. He would have called or texted someone by now.

"No sign of Payton anywhere," said Alex.

"Thanks, guys. Nate, my dad said for us to come home. He's gonna call the police station to find out what's going on."

"Listen, Paris," said Garrett, "we're all worried about Payton too. We'll meet you at your house in a few minutes, okay."

Paris, Leah, and her cousins left 8 Ball and headed to her house. Paris was too nervous to drive and asked Leah to drive her car. Leah obliged.

"Everything is going to be fine, Paris," said Leah. "You know Payton can take care of himself."

"Yeah, I know. But this is not like him. He didn't even call my dad. Something is not right, Leah."

"So where's this police station at?" asked Nate.

"It's on the way home."

"Well, why don't we just go there instead?"

"Good idea, bro. Let's go," said Arianna.

Leah pulled off and headed to the police station.

# *Chapter 13*

They arrived at the police station in twenty minutes or so. As Leah drove up, Paris noticed her dad's car parked right in front. She hoped her dad wouldn't be upset seeing her at the police station. Leah parked the car, and they all went inside the station. Paris saw her parents at the front desk, talking to a police officer.

"What do you mean my son is not here?"

"Mr. Watson," said the officer. "We only had two juvies come in tonight, and neither one is your son."

"Then why don't you tell me where my son is? My daughter said…"

"Dad?" Mr. and Mrs. Watson turned around and saw Paris standing in the doorway.

Mrs. Watson had a worried look on her face and went to hug her daughter. Mr. Watson slightly smiled and walked toward her.

"Sweetie, I told y'all to go home," said her father.

"I know, Dad, but the station was on the way, so we figured to stop by and see if Payton was here."

"Well then, come tell the officer what you told me."

"Sir, there's no need for that. Officer Tilson is on her way up to talk to you and your family. Please have a seat. She'll be right with you."

Mr. Watson and his family sat down and waited for Officer Tilson. Everyone was quiet, not sure what to do or say. All they wanted to know was where was Payton. Paris didn't like how this Christmas was ending up. Just a few short hours ago, everyone was having a good time and enjoying themselves. Now Christmas was taking a turn for the worse. A few minutes later, an Officer entered the lobby.

"Good evening, sir. I'm Officer Tilson. You must be Mr. Watson."

"Yes, I am," said Mr. Watson as he stood up to shake the officer's hand.

"Okay. Well, I need you and your wife to come with me."

"Officer Tilson, my daughter has something to tell you. She knows more about what happened this evening than we do."

"Okay then, young lady, follow me."

Mrs. Watson told Nate to go ahead and take Arianna and Leah home. She hugged her niece and nephew as they left the station. Officer Tilson led the Watsons into a small conference room. As they entered, she grabbed a pen and a legal notebook and placed the items on the table. She reached out her hand to gesture for the Watsons to sit down. The Watsons sat down, and Officer Tilson sat down across from them.

"Okay, young lady, what is your name?"

"Paris Watson."

"Okay, Paris, tell me what happened."

Paris was still nervous and didn't know where to begin. She hesitated for a few minutes. Mrs. Watson gently rubbed Paris's back.

"It's okay, Paris. Just tell the officer what you told your father."

"Okay, Mom. Well, I was at 8 Ball and ready to leave, but I couldn't find my brother Payton, so I asked Chase—"

"Who is Chase?" asked the officer.

"Chase is my friend, and he works at 8 Ball."

"Bartending? Aren't y'all under twenty-one?"

"Most of us are, but they don't serve alcohol, only soda and tea."

"I see. Continue, please..."

"So I asked Chase if he saw my brother, and he said that he saw Payton leave with the security guard. I assumed Payton got arrested and called my dad. Then—"

"So which security guard did you all have working at 8 Ball tonight?" interrupted Mr. Watson.

"Sir, we don't have *any* security guards at this station, just cops here. Paris, sweetie, can you do me a favor and write down your statement on the notepad, just as you told it to me."

"Well, maybe he works at a different station."

"Sir, 8 Ball is in our jurisdiction, and like I said, we don't employ security officers. If there was a security guard there, he may be employed with Security One, which is a local security company that hires cops for security work. I will call them and check for you. I'll be right back."

Officer Tilson left the room to make the call. The Watsons were starting to really worry. Where was Payton, and more importantly, who was he with? Mrs. Watson started to pray for her son. She wouldn't know what to do if anything bad happened to him. Within minutes, Officer Tilson rushed back into the conference room.

"Sir, we just got a call about an accident on the highway. They pulled a security guard out of the car and found a wallet belonging to one Payton Watson in the snow. Come with me. I'll take you all to the hospital."

"What!" yelled Mrs. Watson. "What do you mean an accident?"

"Ma'am, I don't have all the details at the moment, but we need to get to the hospital…now."

Officer Tilson put on her sirens and rushed the Watsons to Memorial Hospital. Mrs. Watson and Paris sat in the back. Paris leaned on her mom and cried. Tears rolled down Mrs. Watson face as she stared at the stars. Mr. Watson sat up front and called his brother.

"Spencer, Payton's been in a car accident. Meet me at the hospital? I'm texting you the address now. See you there."

"Sure thing, bro. We're on our way. By the way, some of Payton's friends are here. What should I tell them?"

Mr. Watson had already hung up the phone. His main concern was getting to the hospital and making sure Payton was okay. He wanted to see the security guard too because if he wasn't dead, Mr. Watson would kill him. No one messes with his family…no one! Just then, Paris got a text.

"Hey, Paris, we're at your house. Where are you?"

"On the way to the hospital."

"Hospital? Why? What happened?"

"Payton was in a car accident Garrett. We don't know anything else."

"Say no more. We're heading there now. See you soon. Payton is a strong dude, and he will be okay. He's going to be fine, Paris."

"Thanks, Garrett. See you soon."

When Officer Tilson arrived at Memorial Hospital, she rushed the Watsons into the emergency entrance and led them to the information desk.

"Excuse me, sir. I'm Officer Tilson, and I received a call a few minutes ago that their son was in an accident and brought here."

"What's the patient's name, Officer Tilson?"

"Payton Watson."

"Are you the parents?" asked the young man.

"Yes, we are," replied Mr. Watson.

"IDs please."

The Watson's handed the clerk their IDs. The young man quickly checked their IDs and told them to have a seat. He picked up the phone and made a call. Within minutes, a doctor met Mr. and Mrs. Watson in the waiting room.

"Are you the boy's father?"

"Yes, Doctor."

"Okay, come with me." The doctor led the Watsons down a hall for privacy.

"Your son was in a very bad accident. Apparently, he didn't have his seat belt on and went through the windshield." Mrs. Watson released a screeching noise. "We had to perform emergency surgery, and your son is still in surgery at the moment. The surgeons are doing their best to help your son."

"I want to see my son," cried Mrs. Watson.

"Ma'am, I'm sorry, but no one is allowed in the surgery room but the surgeons. Please have a seat in the waiting area, and we will keep you updated."

Mr. Watson hugged his wife and led her back to the waiting room where Paris was. The emergency room was quite full, and Mr.

Watson knew that he would be there for a while. He was getting anxious and asked Officer Tilson if she could go find out anything, anything at all. Paris and her mom prayed that Payton's surgery was going well and that they would be able to see him soon.

"Paris, sweetie, can you go get me a cup of coffee? I really could use a nice hot cup of coffee."

"Okay, Mom," sobbed Paris. "I'll be right back."

Mrs. Watson decided that this would be a good time to talk to her husband. Paris would be a few minutes, and their family hadn't reached the hospital yet. She didn't need a lot of time, but she felt a strong urge to get the hurt out of her system. She turned to her husband and started to confess.

"Baby, this is my fault."

"What do you mean, sweetie?"

"I can't hold it in anymore. It's hurting too much."

"What is it, baby?"

"I met him when Paris was three years old. We quickly became friends and started seeing each other on the weekends while you were out of town."

"Are you talking about this Randy guy?"

"Yes, and I think that's who Payton was with."

"How in the world would—"

"Randy's been calling the house, baby. And I think he's been harassing the kids to get to me. I haven't seen or spoken to him in sixteen years, and when I saw him at the house, I knew why he was back. Honey, we spent a lot of time together and—"

"Did you sleep with him?"

Jessica didn't answer.

"Our wedding vows meant nothing to you, huh?"

"That's not true, baby. They meant everything to me. I made a stupid mistake, and I truly regret it. I love you with all my heart, Eric, and I'm very sorry."

"When did the affair end?"

"When you started staying home. And I haven't seen Randy or called him since then."

"So you expect me to believe that you stopped all communications with this guy just like that?"

"Yes, Eric, because it's true."

"Then why the hell did he show up now after some sixteen years?"

"Because when I was about five months pregnant, I bumped into Randy while I was out shopping for the baby. He asked if I was carrying his baby, and I said no. So now I think he's back to find out if Payton is his son."

"You pick a hell of a time to tell me this, Jessica. So are you telling me that you don't know if I'm Payton's father or not?"

"I feel in my heart that Payton is your son, but I—"

"That's enough! I don't want or need to hear anything else. This conversation is over!"

"Can you find it in your heart to forgive me?"

Eric swallowed his tears and heartache. He knew in his heart that he had to forgive Jessica, but at the moment, he just wanted to get away from her. Eric stood up and started to walk away. Jessica grabbed his hand tightly, and he sat back down. He turned to look at her, disgusted. Jessica cupped Eric's cheeks in her hands and rubbed away a tear with her thumb. Eric grabbed Jessica's hand and planted a soft kiss in her palm.

"Baby, right now, all I can think of is Payton and his surgery."

Jessica repeated, "Can you find it in your heart to forgive me?"

Eric didn't answer. He removed Jessica's hands from his face, got up, and walked away. Eric saw Officer Tilson walking toward him. He hurried his steps in her direction.

"Were you able to find out anything?"

"Yes. Unfortunately, the driver didn't make it, so the detectives don't know how the accident happened. Security One does not have a security guard named Randy Brown, so obviously, he's a perp. Your son is still in surgery, and the doctors are doing everything they can to help him. From the looks of it, he's going to be in there for a while. I'm so sorry, sir. Why don't you sit down and relax?"

"Oh my god! What is happening?"

"Mr. Watson, your son is in the best trauma hospital. The doctors here are the best in their field. I'm sure Payton is going to come through just fine. All we can do now is pray and be patient and let the doctors do what they do best. Can I get you anything?"

"No. No, ma'am. And thanks for your concern."

"You're welcome sir. I'll come check on you all soon."

"Thank you. I need to take a walk."

An hour later, Officer Tilson checked on the Watsons. By now, Payton's friends, coaches, and teammates were at the hospital. They were sad and chatting among one another. No one knew what happened to Payton. Leah was consoling Paris. Her uncle Spencer was consoling Arianna, and her aunt Gloria was consoling her mother. Mrs. Watson was crying uncontrollably and wanted to see her son. Payton's friends were trying to stay strong for Payton's family. Mr. Watson finally made his way back to the waiting room and sat down next to his wife. He put his arm around her as she leaned in and rested her head on his chest.

Hours had passed, and a new day was starting. The beautiful brightness of the sun rising woke Mr. Watson. He looked around and noticed that the waiting room was filled with only his family and Payton's friends. Everyone was asleep. He glanced over to his left and noticed that Officer Tilson stayed with his family all night. He knew for sure her shift was over, yet she was still there. He thought that was very thoughtful and caring of her.

"Excuse me, sir," said a tall brown-skinned man in a white lab coat. "Are you Payton's father?"

"Yes. Yes, I am."

"I'm Dr. Shepard, one of the surgeons that worked on Payton. Please come with me." Mr. Watson slowly lifted his wife's head and placed it on her sister's shoulder so he could get up. He followed the doctor down a long and cold corridor.

"Your son's surgery went very well, considering."

"What do you mean?"

"Well, sir, your son suffered major head injuries from being thrown from the vehicle. It took us while to get the swelling down so we could proceed with the surgery. His left leg is broken in two places, and his wrist is severely damaged. He will need extensive rehab while he's here and for a few months thereafter. Fortunately, there was no internal bleeding or damage. It's a miracle that your son survived such a horrific accident. It could have been a lot worse. The angels were with him. They're moving Payton into a private room now, and as soon as he's in there and set up, I will come back and get you and your family."

"Okay, Dr. Shepard. Thank you for taking care of my son. Thank you!"

"My pleasure, sir. I'll see you in a bit."

Mr. Watson made his way back to the waiting room, whispering blessings to God for saving his son. He was then stopped by two detectives. He couldn't wait to speak to them and find out what happened.

"How are you doing, Mr. Watson?" asked one of the detectives.

"Well, I'm okay, considering."

"I'm Detective Matthews, and this is Detective Casey. We've been assigned to your son's case. We're very happy that Payton is out of surgery. Unfortunately, we're unable to speak to him now, so please contact us when he wakes up. We have a few questions to ask him about the accident, and we need to make sure his story lines up with what the other detectives found at the scene."

"Is my son in some kind of trouble?"

"No, sir. We already did some digging and found out that the security guard was not a security guard at all. We just need to tie up some loose ends so we can close the case, sir."

"Oh, I see. I can understand that."

"Oh, by the way, sir. These items were found at the scene." The detective handed Mr. Watson a plastic bag. Inside the bag was Payton's wallet, cell phone, and a gold envelope. "We figured these items must be your son's since the wallet is his."

"Thank you, Detectives."

"No problem. Please, the moment he wakes, give us a call."

The detectives made their way through the waiting room and out the door. Mr. Watson watched them as they left and then turned his attention to the plastic bag. *What is this?* he thought. He pulled the gold envelope out of the bag and saw the address on it, Courts of Child Welfare, Paternity Division. *What the hell is this? Was Payton trying to get this from the officer?* He wanted to open the package but knew deep down inside that he didn't want to know what the documents revealed. Mr. Watson knew in his heart that Payton was his son. Every time he looked at Payton, he saw himself when he was Payton's age. Every time Payton smiled, he saw his wife's smile. And every time he felt the warmth of his son, he knew Payton had the same good heart as he did. No documents were going to tell him otherwise. Mr. Watson made his way to the triage station and asked the nurse if she could shred the envelope. Without any hesitation, she got up and shredded the gold envelope. Mr. Watson made his way back to the waiting room. Mrs. Watson was awake and drinking coffee.

"Hey, baby, where'd you go?"

"I went for a walk and then had a talk with the doctor. He said the surgery went well, and they are moving Payton into a private room."

"Praise God," said Jessica.

"When he's all set up in the room, the doctor is going to come and get us. Now how are you doing?"

"I'm doing okay. I just feel so ashamed, and I feel terrible for hurting you. I'm so sorry."

"Jessica, baby, I love you. You and the kids are my life. We have a beautiful family, and look around you, your son is a good person. His friends and teammates stayed here all night. I know Payton has a good heart, and my heart is telling me all I need to know, that Payton is my *son*! And yes, I forgive you."

"I'm so sorry, baby."

"Baby, it's a new day. Let's just be thankful that God spared our son."

Eric kissed his wife and hugged her tightly. Jessica hugged Eric even tighter and didn't want to let go. Eric figured Jessica would never have to know about the documents and the destruction of them. It didn't matter. All that mattered now was that his only son was alive.

"Excuse me, sir," said a young nurse. "Your son is in his room now. He's heavily sedated and asleep, but you two can see him now. Follow me."

Mr. and Mrs. Watson held hands as they followed the nurse to Payton's room. They didn't know what to expect, but they felt blessed that Payton was alive.

# Chapter 14

Mr. and Mrs. Watson entered Payton's room and hurried to his bedside. He didn't look like their son at all. He was bandaged up pretty badly, his leg was in a sling, and his head was wrapped in white bandages. Mrs. Watson pulled a chair next to the bed and gently grabbed her son's hand. He was so cold. Mr. Watson walked around the bed and grabbed Payton's other hand. The Watson's then grabbed each other's hand and prayed over Payton. They knew that the Lord would hear their prayers and heal their son.

"Baby, look at him," said Mrs. Watson. "I can't believe this is my son. He's so helpless right now, and I can't even hug him."

"Sweetie, don't worry. He's alive. Let's just pray he wakes up soon."

Mrs. Watson put her head down on Payton's forearm and quietly cried. She was over tired now, and all she wanted to do was go back to sleep, but she couldn't. All she could think about was Payton. And although he was alive, she couldn't help but think that this was all her fault. She should have never brought another man into her home. She knew it was wrong from the day she met Randy, but she let her emotions take over and thought she would be able to handle it. Now her only son was lying in a hospital with life-threatening injuries."

"Baby, look, he's waking up."

"Hey, Payton, baby," his mother said softly. "We've been waiting for you to wake up. Can you hear me?"

Payton barely nodded. He couldn't talk with the tube in his mouth, and he couldn't move at all. His eyes slowly moved back and forth. Then they slowly closed again.

"Baby, you were in a car accident. You're in the hospital now, and everything is going to be okay."

Payton slowly opened his eyes, and a tear rolled down his cheek. His parents saw in his face that Payton wanted to talk, as if he had to get something out.

Mrs. Watson wiped the tear from Payton's cheek and smiled. She then got up and kissed her son on his forehead as she wiped a tear from her own cheek.

"Sweetie, can you go see if Paris is up? I'm sure she will want to see Payton."

"Sure, baby. I'll be right back."

Mr. Watson left the room and made his way to the waiting room. He stopped at a window on the way to the waiting room and noticed that it was a beautiful December day. Even on this cold day, the sun was shining extremely bright. "Thank you, Jesus," whispered Mr. Watson. "Thank you for saving my son!"

"Dad, Dad," said Paris from a few feet away.

Mr. Watson turned around and saw Paris and another young lady walking toward him.

"Yes, honey?"

"How's Payton? Where is he?"

"Payton's fine, sweetie. He's in his room now. I was just on my way to get you. I have to warn you, though, he's pretty banged up and doesn't look like your brother."

"Well, I wanna see him. Can you take us to his room?"

"Follow me."

Mr. Watson led the girls to Payton's room. When they entered, Paris's eyes raced to Payton's bed, and she couldn't believe what she saw. Paris covered her mouth, and started to cry. Mr. Watson hugged Paris and walked her to Payton's bedside. Paris tried to wipe the tears from her eyes before she reached Payton, but she was unsuccessful. Paris's eyes met Payton's, and at that moment, she saw the strength of her brother. She knew then that Payton was going to be fine. She smiled, leaned in, and kissed Payton on the cheek.

Payton saw Tiffany standing a few feet behind Paris. She was sniffling and trying to hold her composure, but as she reached

Payton's side and saw the condition he was in, she cried softly. With his one good arm, he slowly lifted his hand and waved at Tiffany to come closer. Tiffany wasn't sure if she wanted to get any closer. She started to walk toward Payton, but she hesitated. Payton motioned again for Tiffany to come closer. Tiffany slowly made her way to his side, and with tears in her eyes, she gently touched Payton's hand. Payton slowly lifted Tiffany's hand and locked his fingers in hers as a tear rolled down his cheek. He wanted to wipe Tiffany's tears away and couldn't. He wanted to hug and hold Tiffany, but he couldn't. And most of all, Payton wanted to kiss Tiffany again, but he couldn't.

Tiffany lifted Payton's hand and kissed it. She knew it was time to answer his question.

"Yes, Payton, we can get to know each other better!"

THE END

# *About the Author*

Karon was born and raised in the small town of Bayonne, New Jersey. She attended Henry E. Harris elementary school and later Bayonne High School. After graduating Bayonne High School with honors, she was determined to further her education. She enrolled at Jersey City State College, where she majored in Business Management. In 1992, she graduated from JCSC, earning her bachelors of science degree in business. Her love for writing began when she was a young girl. She finds pleasure and happiness in writing. Being able to put her thoughts and imagination into words that she could share with others gives her a quiet sense of gratification. As she delivers her first published book, she hopes to share her joy, laughter, and tears of writing with all her readers around the world.

CPSIA information can be obtained
at www.ICGtesting.com
Printed in the USA
BVHW071620170921
616961BV00003B/300